Evarts Scudder, Charles Allen Sumner

Memorial Record in Memory of Honourable Increase

Sumner of Great Barrington, Mass.

Evarts Scudder, Charles Allen Sumner

Memorial Record in Memory of Honourable Increase Sumner of Great Barrington, Mass.

ISBN/EAN: 9783337817459

Printed in Europe, USA, Canada, Australia, Japan

Cover: Foto ©Raphael Reischuk / pixelio.de

More available books at **www.hansebooks.com**

MEMORIAL RECORD.

IN MEMORY

OF

HON. INCREASE SUMNER,

OF GREAT BARRINGTON, MASS.

A FUNERAL DISCOURSE,

BY

REV. EVARTS SCUDDER.

WITH

AN APPENDIX,

CONTAINING

OBITUARY NOTICES OF THE PRESS; RESOLUTIONS
AND PROCEEDINGS OF THE BERKSHIRE BAR;
AND DEDICATORY EXERCISES OF
JULIA SUMNER HALL.

BRIDGEPORT, CONN.:
GOULD & STILES, (FARMER OFFICE,) COR. WALL AND WATER STS.

1871.

S.ERMON.

Job 3: 19.—"The small and the great are there."

In the hour of this nation's sorest need, when the powers of darkness seemed to be almost triumphant, our President was suddenly struck down by Death. Upon the day of his funeral while nearly the whole nation were in tears, I carried to the grave the body of a little boy who was unknown by many in his own native village. Looking into the grave upon that day we realized the truth of Job's words : " The small and the great are there." " They shall lie down alike together." The dust of one is as good as the dust of another. There is no wealth in the grave. Kings leave their sceptres. Master and slave meet there and know no distinction. The idiot and the scholar, the beggar and the millionaire, the small and the great are there. Death hesitates not to bid the man of business lay down his ledger, the warrior his sword, or the judge his ermine. No insignia of rank, or marks of beauty, or proofs of usefulness stop him as he summons his followers, one by one, and marches on. O what a mighty host is the army that he gathers !

How its ranks increase as they follow their mighty captain obediently, silently, and swiftly from house to house, to palace and hovel, to the battle-field, to hospital and to prison, now to some far off vessel upon the sea, and then to the crowded city or country village, making no distinction, granting no discharge, inexorable, irresistible—the long invisible army of the dead !

The inexorable demand of Death appears more striking when we think of the hopes which some cherish of avoiding death. Some imagine that *youth* will necessarily exempt them from Death's call. But a larger number die in youth than in old age. How often those who seem to have a reasonable hope of a long life are suddenly summoned by Death. Some youth in this assembly with perfect health, vigorous, temperate and expecting to live long, whom an insurance company would unhesitatingly insure for almost any amount, may be the next one obliged to die. " Boast not thyself of to-morrow."

Usefulness does not hinder Death. Yet many imagine that they, or some friend of theirs, cannot be spared just yet from earth. The thought of work to be done, of unfinished plans, of influence for good impresses them with the feeling that their appointed time is not at hand. They reason thus : " God has put me here for some purpose. The days of our years are three score years and ten. It takes as long as that to accomplish much of anything. Even with the future life to compensate for this, may I not reasonably expect to live out the full measure of my days ? What does a life amount to that is cut off just as it is begun !" So we reason ; but God's thoughts are not as ours, and He often destroys man's hope. The most useful, those whom the world seems to need the most, whose influence, conscious or unconscious, is most positively good, the friends of every good enterprise, the friends of virtue and of peace, the friends of the poor, those fitted by natural endowment and culture to fill any office of trust and power, how often are these shining marks for Death's arrows! The most useful as well as the youngest, are often the very ones whom Death is most eager for.

You need not be reminded that *love* is no protection against Death. Those loved the most, to whom we cling with the tenderest affection, those leaned upon, or because of some infirmity cared for with sleepless vigilance, these, O how certain to be summoned away just when we loved and needed them the most!

" But if Death hesitates not at a man's door for any other reason, surely that man's *religious character* is a matter which Death takes into consideration, is it not?" We answer, No. It makes no difference how much or how little goodness a person may then have. He may be a spiritual millionaire, or the veriest pauper in morals ; he may be like a garden full of weeds and the seeds of weeds, with no room for one blade of honest grass ; and yet Death will not wait for one weed more to be rooted out, or for one flower more to blossom. " It is *appointed* unto man once to die." The day for Death to dismount from his pale horse and to knock at your door, or at mine, is already chosen ; and when that day comes it will make no difference with him whether we have lived as we ought to live or not. We may then be illustrious for virtue of every hue, or we may be the talk of the town for the faults and vices that we are guilty of ; we may have fought successfully many a hard battle with sin, or we may have skulked away and even have sold ourselves to the enemy; nevertheless, when that appointed hour strikes, Death will be at our door, and no bar or bolt can keep him out. My friend, at that moment, which will soon be here, you may have arranged your affairs without having made any preparation for the last and greatest duty—the duty of dying. You may then be utterly unready, with everything to see to, and yet it will not make one second's difference with that unrelenting messenger of God. No entreaty will avail with him. No excuse will delay his coming. He may surprise you in the midst of important work ; you may be just entering your closet for the first time to pray ; but he will not wait for you to pray—he will not wait for you to give yourself to God. Why should he? Have you not had time to prepare for death? Have you not had warning? Has not God spoken in His word and in His providence? Have you not heard the gospel? Have you not read the Bible? Well may Death himself be startled not to find you ready, and he might exclaim : " Have you not seen the notice of my coming, printed on every gravestone, sounded by every church-bell, repeated at every funeral, by every sermon, by every ache and pain in your body, preached to you by every setting sun and falling leaf? Not ready for my coming! Why, how old art thou? Twenty? thirty-five? sixty years? and still unprepared to die! It matters not—this warrant I must serve !" And, my friend, his summons you will obey.

This fact, that there can be no postponement of Death's coming when the appointed hour arrives; that no condition in life and no type of character can avert or delay the execution of that sentence of death passed upon all men, ought to convince every one that a preparation for death consists in something else than a good character and a holy life.

The impression with many is, that one must prepare for death by a long and faithful struggle with faults; that the character must be pruned and ripened; that one must at least have got the better of besetting sins, and must have earned, in the estimation of his fellow-men a fair title to the heavenly inheritance; that he must be able to present an argument at the bar of God's judgment for his own acquittal, based upon at least a respectable degree of good intention. But such a preparation is utterly impossible. If a right moral character be the necessary preparation for death, God's perfect law is the only test of that preparation; but we read—" He that offendeth in one point is guilty of all," and also that " all have sinned and come short of the glory of God." . Now, where is the man who can stand the test of God's perfect law ? Who is there " perfect as our Father in heaven is perfect ?" What one of you would dare stand to-day at God's bar, and plead, " Not guilty ?" Though you may have kept God's law to-day, there is the sin of yesterday ! The sins of all the past, are they not witnesses against you, and do they not prove you unprepared to die ?

Moreover, if right living be the true and only preparation for God's final judgment of us, why does not Death give all an equal chance ? What means it that Death is so unyielding in his demands, and bids man put on his white livery and depart at once, whether he be ready or not ? Why does not Death give every man a full opportunity of making the necessary preparation, by overcoming sin and perfecting a character which will be able to stand God's scrutiny ?   Here is one who is beginning in good earnest to repent of sin, but he is full of faults ; sin is rooted in him ; and his heart is all tied up by bad habits.   Why does not Death postpone his coming to that soul, if eternity can be prepared for only by the possession of a spotless character.

Thank God ! the reason is, that to be saved, one need only trust in the Lord Jesus Christ—God's Son—who died that sinful men might, in spite of their sin, be ready for Death's summons, however early and however suddenly he might come.   This is the preparation to be made.   " Other foundation can no man lay."   " He that believeth shall be saved."   " Who shall lay anything to the charge of God's elect ?   It is God that justifieth.   Who is he that condemneth ?   It is Christ that died."   *This* is the argument with which to plead successfully at God's judgment bar *Not* the argument from a holy life ; *not* the argument from a tolerably respectable and average morality ; *not* that from good intentions—but the argument based upon the atonement and mediation of the Son of God.   This argument begins by pleading guilty and admitting all the counts in the accusation.   The accused *is* a sinner and does not pretend to deserve one iota of God's favor.   He cannot contradict or excuse the facts.   Yet he has one plea which never has failed and which never can fail, because God bids him make it,—the plea that Jesus died *for him* upon the cross.   He who is ready to go before God with this, and only this ground of hope, is prepared to die.   He has retained Jesus Christ as his advocate, and therefore may quietly await the summons of God's High Sheriff, Death.

Friends : to just this preparation we all are limited. Whoever we may be ; however we may have lived ; however nobly, usefully, beautifully ; whether we be rich, or learned, or eloquent,. or famous, or quite the reverse ; whether we go to the grave " unwept, unhonored and un- sung," or followed by a throng of weeping friends, lamented by the whole nation it may be ; our hope can only be in the grace of Jesus Christ, God's Son. Answering Death's summons, the soul in readiness replies :

"Just as I am, without one plea,
But that thy blood was shed for me,
And that thou bid'st me come to thee:
O Lamb of God, I come."

We have directed your attention to this thought partly because it was this that occupied and comforted our friend in his last sickness. *Judge Sumner*, after nearly seventy years' experience, about fifty of which were spent in pro- fessional study and practice, accustomed to measure the character and to test the motives of men, intelligent and honest, emphatically said that his life had been " far differ- ent from what it should have been," and that his hope was " only in the mercy of God through the mediation of His Son."

There was much to admire in his life and character. His self-education, for he was graduated at no college ; his great physical vigor and untiring industry ; his wonderful memory; his legal learning and his success as a lawyer ; his perfect integrity in all public office ; his friendliness to the poor ; his hatred of meanness and dishonesty ; his warm and generous love for his family and friends ; these facts and traits rendered him worthy of the respect felt by all who

2

knew him well. His long, successful, useful and honorable career, should encourage every other farmer boy on our New England hills to a similar hope and effort.

But all his honors, all success that he had had, and his whole influence as a man and lawyer, he desired to lay down at the feet of Jesus Christ, and to take his place with the very worst criminal as a guilty, sinful and unworthy man; hoping, as he himself said, "only in the mercy of God through the mediation of Jesus Christ, His Son."

I know that he had faults—(who has not?)—many faults it may be, and he was ready to admit them; faults which his professional conflict with men was not fitted to disguise or soften; faults which, as he was a public man, subjected him to criticism and to the enmity of some; faults arising from a nervous and impulsive nature, which he did not conceal or resist as he ought to have done. All this I know, but as I remember them I also recall the words of the Master: "Judge not that *ye* be not judged."

I was sent for by him early one morning during his last sickness, and as I sat there by his bedside, I felt that it was an honest hour, and that I could believe him when, in various words, he told me that his hope was in the Saviour. "Only there," he said, "only there!" "O what a Saviour he is!" was his repeated exclamation. As I listened to his clear and earnest words about death, about the Saviour, I could not help wishing that he had stood up before men and plead the cause of Christ as ably and eloquently as he used to plead the cause of men. But I felt that the hour of death is an honest hour. That was with him an honest hour also, I think, at midnight on last New Year's eve. The clock struck twelve, and the new year began. He noticed it with pleasant words of reminiscence and hope, and deeply impressed as he lay awake in that first hour of 1871, he said, " Let us pray the prayer our Lord taught his disciples." Thus *he* began the year.

[Since the above was written I have learned that at one time in his sickness when he was encouraged by the hope of recovery, he said, referring to the hour when he had seemed to be very near death, " I stood upon the brink and it would have been just as easy to step over to the other side as to step back—there was no pain and no fear." He talked much to his wife of God's mercy to him—" I have passed through great sorrow—four children gone—*you* know what it was for me to part with one of them—and a sorrow beyond that. But God has been kind to me through it all."]

As the sun was going down, last Friday afternoon, I entered his home and found that the sunset of his life was just at hand. His three score years and ten were nearly ended—and as he quietly breathed his last, we knelt down and prayed, " Lord Jesus receive his spirit." With that Lord we leave him, as we ourselves must be left by those who shall weep for us. And we can leave him so, for that Lord does all things well.

APPENDIX.

NOTICES OF THE PRESS.

From the Pittsfield Sun, February 16th, 1871.

THE LATE JUDGE SUMNER.

INCREASE SUMNER was born at Otis, May 13th, 1801. His father was Daniel Sumner, a native of Middletown, Conn., and one of the early settlers of Otis. He had a family of seven children, of whom Increase was the fifth. He had but limited opportunities for early education, but early developed a taste for study, in which he was encouraged by an older brother, who was a medical student, and afterwards an esteemed physician.

In 1820, Increase became a law-student in the office of Hon. Lester Filley at Otis, where he remained for a period of five years, during a considerable of which time he was engaged in teaching school as a means of paying his way.

He taught school in Otis and in Sandisfield, and in the towns of Kinderhook and Cambridge in the State of New York.

In 1825 he removed to Great-Barrington. He had intended to locate in Springfield, and always deemed it the mistake of his life-time that he did not do so; but the removal from Great-Barrington of William C. Bryant created a vacancy there, and Mr. Sumner was his successor as it were. Several of the law books in his library bear the autograph of William C. Bryant.

The record of Mr. Sumner's career as a lawyer is best shown in the law reports of the State, extending over a period of forty years, and is familiar to the profession. His practice was not restricted within State lines, and he tried many causes in the neighboring States of New York and Connecticut.

Mr. Sumner was twice a State Senator, and declined another election when his party was predominant, and he would undoubtedly have been President of the Senate. He was three times a member of the House of Representatives, the last time being in 1859, when the General Statutes were revised, and the position of Mr. Sumner on the Judiciary Committee was such that more labor devolved upon him in connection with that Revision than upon any other member of that Legislature.

He was Democratic candidate for Congress in 1844, his successful competitor being the Whig candidate, Hon. Julius Rockwell.

In 1851 he was appointed by Governor Boutwell, District Attorney of the Western District of Massachusetts, then comprising four Counties, and served as such two years.

In 1853 he was elected to represent his native town, Otis, in the Constitutional Convention. He was three times a candidate of the Republican and American parties for the office of Lieutenant-Governor, and in 1856 was Delegate to the Convention at Philadelphia which nominated Millard Fillmore for President.

During the early part of his career he held various town offices; and was Postmaster at Great-Barrington during the Van Buren and Tyler administrations.

In 1849 he was appointed by Governor Briggs one of the Commissioners on the part of Massachusetts to negotiate with Commissioners of Rhode Island for settlement of the boundary line between those States. His associates were Tappan Wentworth of Lowell, and N. B. Bryant of Barre.

In 1854 he was appointed by Governor Washburne to act with Levi Lincoln of Worcester, and Edward Jarvis of Dorchester, as a Commission to investigate the condition of the State institutions for Insane and Idiotic persons, and to report a plan and location for a new Hospital. Much time and labor were expended in performing the duties of this commission, and the Report made by it was published by order of the Legislature, making a volume of 200 pages.

The last public office held by Mr. Sumner was that of Judge of the District Court of Southern Berkshire, to which he was appointed by Governor Claflin to hold for life, and which position he occupied at the time of his decease.

Judge Sumner's career throughout was remarkable for singular devotion to the duties of his profession. He was a born lawyer, and loved his calling. He never slighted a cause, and always took the laboring oar, when others were associated with him.

The files of the Berkshire Courts embrace more matter in his hand-writing than in that of any other lawyer at the bar, except the County Clerks, since the Bar of Berkshire had an existence. He was not only learned as a lawyer, but eloquent as an advocate. He was a dangerous antagonist before a jury.

Aside from his legal and official labors, he found time for other congenial pursuits. He had fine literary tastes. At one period of his life he wrote many poetical effusions, several of which were published. His orations and addresses, on political, agricultural and literary topics, would fill volumes. He accumulated a large miscellaneous library, in which none of the really standard works were missing. No man was better acquainted with such authors as Bacon and Burke than he. Whatever defects might have existed in his early education were obviated by subsequent study, and his scholarly attainments were recognized by the Corporation of Williams College in 1839, when that institution conferred upon him the honorary degree of Master of Arts.

The Chapter in the published Life of Governor Briggs, relating to the Governor's career at the Bar, was written by Mr. Sumner, and the whole work would have been prepared by him and under his supervision, if his professional engagements had left him leisure to assume the undertaking.

In his private life Judge Sumner was a man of singular integrity, and in all his dealings, above reproach. In the community where he lived he had no peers, and by some he was regarded, perhaps justly, as too brusque in his manner, and imperious in his bearing. Had he lived in the midst of a large community, these little characteristics would have passed unnoticed. In his domestic relations he was kind and tender, and among his neighbors

> " Lofty and sour to those who loved him not,
> But unto such as sought him, sweet as summer."

But those who loved him least, will not hesitate to allow, that although there might have been something of the tiger in his composition, there was nothing of the *snake*. What he thought, he made people understand, but there was no double-facedness about him. For the mean man he had intense disgust, and to the man who dealt dishonestly he was ever a terror.

Among his brethren at the Bar, Judge Sumner was regarded with more than respect and admiration. It was with affection. At the recent Bar Meeting and Banquet, he was chosen by acclamation to preside, and that last meeting of his with his legal brethren cannot but be regarded as a fitting culmination of his long, laborious and successful professional career.

He died, having been less honored perhaps in his life than accorded with his deserts, but highly esteemed by those whose esteem was most valuable. Lesser men have held higher place, but it is believed that he is sincerely mourned, and that the best of those who knew him best will mourn him most.

From the Berkshire County Eagle, February 2d, 1871.

THE HON. INCREASE SUMNER.

After an illness of four weeks, the Honorable Increase Sumner, the oldest member of the Berkshire Bar, died at his home in Great-Barrington, on Friday last, aged 70 years.

Mr. Sumner was born in Otis, May 13th, 1801. He studied law for seven years (the time then required of those who were not college graduates), with Lester Filley, Esq., of Otis. On his admission to the Bar, at the June Term, 1825, he removed to Great-Barrington, where he resided until his death. He was always an active and successful practitioner, and for a long time has been the acknowledged leader of the Berkshire Bar. Although, as the phrase is, self-educated, he was a man of superior culture, and familiar, not only with the learning of his profession but with general literature and science. A man of strong convictions, and deep thought, yet he was not ashamed to change party ties when he thought he had good reason for so doing. In Van Buren times he was a Democrat; afterward was associated

3

with the American party, and later became a strong supporter of the Republican party.   He had served often in both branches of the State Legislature;
been nominated more than once for Congress; succeeded Mr. Porter of Lee,
as District Attorney for the Western District; was a member, elected from
Otis, of the late Constitutional Convention, and once served on a State Commission to investigate the causes of insanity and the treatment of the insane.
His latest office, that of Judge of the District Court of Southern Berkshire,
was given him within the year.   Mr. Sumner was twice married.   His first
wife was Miss Barstow of Great-Barrington.   He leaves three sons—children
by his first wife—Col. Samuel B. Sumner of Bridgeport, and Charles and
Albert, both of whom reside in California.   His second wife was a Boston
lady, who survives him.

When Mr. Sumner's death was announced on Saturday, in his own Court,
a meeting of the Bar present was held, and a committee appointed to draft
suitable resolutions, which will be reported on Saturday.   The District
Court of Central Berkshire also adjourned as a mark of respect to his memory.
His funeral was attended on Tuesday.   The services were a prayer at the
house, and the usual services at the Congregational Church, and the burial
service at the grave.   The funeral sermon was preached by the Rev. Mr.
Scudder of Great-Barrington, from Job 3: 19—" The small and the great are
there"—and was a most eloquent and fitting discourse.   Mr. Scudder was
assisted by Rev. Mr. Maxcy of Bridgeport, and Rev. Dr. Olmstead of Great-
Barrington.   The places of business in the town were closed, and a very
large concourse attended the services in the church.

High Sheriff Root and quite a number of deputies were present at the
funeral, and the Bar of Berkshire was strongly represented.   The pall bearers
were Hon. George J. Tucker of Lenox, Hon. James D. Colt of Pittsfield,
Hon. M. Wilcox of Pittsfield, H. J. Bliss, Esq. of North Adams, L. H. Gam-
well, Esq., of Pittsfield, Hon. John Branning of Lee.   Other members of the
Bar present were Messrs. Dewey and Palmer of Great-Barrington, Bradford
of Sheffield, Spaulding of West Stockbridge, Taft and Waterman of Lenox,
Goodrich of Stockbridge, Filley, Pingree, Adam, Barker, Tatlock and Briggs
of Pittsfield.

From the Alta California, February 19th, 1871.

DEATH OF INCREASE SUMNER.

Reminiscences of the Old Berkshire Bar—High Tributes in
Memory of One who for a Long Time was its Leading Advocate.

From the Adams Transcript and Berkshire Courier, we copy the subjoined
records in regard to the life and character of the eminent lawyer, Judge Increase Sumner, who died at Great-Barrington, Mass., on the 27th of January
last.   He was well known to a large number of the members of the bar in

this State, some of whom studied law in his office; and he leaves two sons who reside in this city.

The Adams Transcript of February 6th, says:

" The death of this eminent member of the Berkshire Bar occurred on Friday week, at the ripe age of 70 years. He had long been in feeble health, and at the recent Bar Festival in Pittsfield, the signs of age and ill-health were noticed by all, although his speech was marked by intellectual power and clearness. He died of typhoid fever, after a sickness of several weeks. At the time of his death he was Judge of the District Court of Southern Berkshire, and the oldest lawyer but one of the Bar. He was the last active member of that influential and distinguished group of men who ruled the Berkshire Bar twenty-five years ago. We can recall but five survivors— Sayles of South Adams, the Tucker brothers, and Judges Rockwell and Bishop of Lenox, and all of these, except Sayles, long since abandoned active practice. Sumner has now gone to join in the 'silent land' his associates and compeers—Briggs, Byington, Dwight, Whiting, Hubbard, Filley, Robinson, Field, Porter, Dewey and Lanckton. That was a notable circle of strong men, who used to contend in the lists at the old court-house at Lenox, and who, after the struggles of the day were over, and they had reached the parlor of the Curtis boarding house across the way, made the nights delightful and memorable with their sparkling stories and converse. Those were brilliant days and nights for the younger members of the bar, who never wearied at these rare and stimulating exhibitions of power and wit. Time and fate have changed all this, and rapidly removed these actors from mortal view. Among this famous company, Mr. Sumner was conspicuous for his legal learning, his skill and eloquence as an advocate, his tireless energy and indomitable will and courage in the conduct of causes. He was fond of social converse, and before ill-health and trouble had weakened him, he furnished an important contribution to the common enjoyment. He had failings and infirmities, like the rest, but these are now forgotten as we remember the stalwart will, the eloquent tongue, the keen wit, the robust conquering logic of this remarkable pleader. He loved the profession and devoted all his faculties to its practice. He was true to his clients, and fought for their interests with unquenchable ardor, and, for a long time, was the leader of the bar. Those who heard him in his prime, will not soon forget that rare forensic skill and powerful speech."

The Berkshire Courier of the 8th, gives the following account of proceedings in the District Court of Southern Berkshire, in respect to the memory of Judge Sumner:

" In this Court on Saturday, January 28th, as soon as the necessary business of entering and continuing cases was dispatched (Judge Bradford presiding), Mr. Wilcox of Pittsfield, referred to the recent death of Hon. Increase Sumner, the late standing Justice of said court, and expressed his respect for the character, ability and attainments of the deceased, alluded to some of the qualities which had enabled him to hold, for so long a time, a commanding position in Western Massachusetts, and closed by suggesting to the Court that a committee be appointed to draw up some resolutions, embodying in permanent form the feelings of those present toward Mr. Sumner, which resolutions should be reported at the next session of the Court and be entered on its records. Messrs. Branning of Lee, and Dewey of Great-Barrington, supported these suggestions, and Judge Bradford, after speaking briefly but eloquently of Mr. Sumner, appointed Messrs. Wilcox, Branning and Dewey as Committee. The Court, as a mark of respect to the deceased, then adjourned. On Saturday, February 4th, the Committee, through the chairman, Mr. Wilcox, presented to the Court the following resolutions:

"RESOLVED, That in the decease of the Honorable INCREASE SUMNER, the community is bereaved of a valued and honored citizen, and the Bar of one of its ablest members, and this Court of its first Chief Magistrate. For half a century, nearly, he was a man of mark and commanding influence, not in the town of his early adoption and long residence only, but throughout this community and wherever known. And during the same period his career at the bar, in this his native county, suffers nothing in comparison with that of his distinguished compeers, Dwight, Briggs, Byington, Filley and Robinson, and others who have preceded him to the spirit land.

"He by nature was fitted for prominence and a leader in any community and at any bar.

"His efforts, whether before the jury or the Court, were always able, and at times rose to an eloquence rarely surpassed. His integrity was never questioned. He possessed great industry, logic and a sound judgment as well as eloquence, which, united with his characteristic fidelity and invincible will, achieved for him as a lawyer a position second to none in the history of the bar of Berkshire. He loved his profession, and practiced it with unabated zeal to the very last of life, and died ripe in years, having scarcely laid his brief aside.

"RESOLVED, That the decease of such a man, even though full of years and crowned with success, is no ordinary event, and well may we of the Bar surviving him study his example. if we would practice and emulate, his virtues.

"RESOLVED, That we extend to the widow, and family of the deceased, our hearty sympathies; and that these resolutions be extended upon the records of this Court, and a copy thereof presented to his family.

"Judge Bradford said that in compliance with the terms of the resolutions he would cause the same to be entered at once on the records of the Court, and a copy to be furnished to the family of the deceased. At the presentation of the resolutions, brief remarks were made by Mr. Wilcox only, it being the understanding of the members of the bar present, that the death of Mr. Sumner would be made the occasion for a meeting of the entire bar of the county, at which time all, individually by personal speech, and collectively by resolutions, could express their respect to the memory of Mr. Sumner, and their estimate of his character and work."

JUDGE SUMNER'S DEATH.—THE DISTRICT COURT OF CENTRAL BERKSHIRE.

News of the death of Judge Increase Sumner, of Great-Barrington was received in town on Saturday. The District Court was in session, but on motion of T. P. Pingree, Esq., it adjourned. The motion to adjourn was as follows:

To the Honorable, the District Court of Central Berkshire, its Judges and Officers:

The decease of our honored and distinguished brother at the Bar, Increase Sumner of Great-Barrington, the 27th instant, calls for some token on our part, of respect to his memory, and grief for our loss, as the public's generally, in the removal of so upright and able an officer of the Court, and such an example of integrity and faithfulness in the practice of the profession of law, as also in its administration as a Judge of a sister Court in this county.

Therefore, it is moved that this Court do now adjourn, as an expression on its part, of the sincerity of respect and esteem entertained for our late brother, and that this motion, with other expressions of like kind in writing, be placed on file and entered on the Docket.

Pittsfield, January 30th, 1871.   T. P. PINGREE.

J. M. Barker, Esq., in seconding the motion, said:

It is with feelings of profound sadness, that I this morning, hear announced to your Honor the death of our elder brother and leader, Increase Sumner, of Great-Barrington. Himself a wearer of the ermine, it is doubly fitting that some record should be made in your Honor's Court, of the departure of so upright a judge, and so sound and able a lawyer.

The Superior Courts of Judicature will claim the right to enroll upon their records, and the whole Bar to move the usual expressions of admiration for the man; of regret at his loss, and of sympathy and condolence with the family of which he was the head.

But it is right and proper for the District Court of Central Berkshire, to take official notice of the death of the Justice of its sister Court, and it is not presumptuous for the bar of the County seat to add an expression of their sorrow for the loss of the lawyer, whose acknowledged talent and ripe experience claimed and received our highest admiration and respect. It is not too much to say that for years our juries have been accustomed to listen with delight to his eloquence, our courts to receive his words as carrying weighty sanction in the law, and ourselves to study his conduct and efforts at the bar, as our best examples of professional skill and learning, while his large circle of clients ever found in his perfect integrity a sure protection.

Judge Sumner died yesterday at his home in Great-Barrington. It is but a few weeks—a month ago to-day—that, called by one thought of all to be President of our Bar Association, he presided at our Annual Dinner, filled with the enthusiasm and genius, which had made his name so widely known and honored. Now the flashing eye is closed forever, the shapely hand of the orator is still, and the venerable head laid low in death. But the bright soul freed from the tenement of clay soars untrammeled, and the record of a life well spent remains as a legacy to us all. I have no qualification, may it please your Honor, which renders it proper for me to call your attention to our brother's death, except a deep respect and admiration for the deceased, and a lively gratitude for his uniform courtesy to the younger members of the bar, and I will therefore trespass no longer on your indulgence, or that of my brothers, save to second the motion that a minute of Judge Sumner's death be entered upon the record, and that the Court do stand adjourned in token of respect to his memory.

SUPERIOR COURT PROCEEDINGS.

At the February Term, 1871, of the Superior Court, in Pittsfield, appropriate action was taken in regard to the death of the Hon. Increase Sumner of Great-Barrington, for forty-five years a member of the Berkshire Bar. The subjoined resolutions were presented:

"At a meeting of the members of the Berkshire Bar, held this 28th day of February, 1871, Henry W. Taft, Franklin O. Sayles, Wm. T. Filley, Marshall Wilcox and Justin Dewey, Jr., were appointed a Committee to prepare suitable resolutions to be presented to the Superior Court now in session, upon the occasion of the recent death of the Hon. Increase Sumner, late of Great-Barrington. And in discharge of that duty the Committee present to the Court the following resolutions:

"RESOLVED, That the members of the Berkshire Bar, while humbly acknowledging the wisdom and kindness of all the dispensations of Divine Providence, desire here to express and record their profound sorrow, that death has deprived them of the counsels and companionship of their brother, so recently deceased, the Hon. Increase Sumner of Great-Barrington.

" RESOLVED, That resolutions such as these, proper to be adopted when any member of the Bar passes away from the earthly fellowship of his brethren, may well be attended with an expression of peculiar regard and affectionate respect, when one like Mr. Sumner has taken leave of his profession and his life at the same time, after an almost entire devotion to the duties of that profession, for a period of forty-five years, discharging those duties always with fidelity, industry, and extraordinary gifts of intellect and eloquence.

" RESOLVED, That the career of our late associate, in many respects, may well be referred to, as an example to young men of our honorable profession, and of every profession and occupation—particularly as showing the important and comforting truth, that inherited wealth is not necessary to success in life—but that industry and a resolute will can more than supply its place.

" RESOLVED, That we respectfully request of the Honorable Charles Devens, Jr., the Judge presiding at this term, to allow these resolutions to be placed upon the records of the Court, and to direct that a copy thereof, attested by the Clerk, may be transmitted to the widow and family of the deceased."

These resolutions, at the request of the Committee, were presented by Judge JULIUS ROCKWELL, with the following remarks, in substance:

MAY IT PLEASE THE COURT:

I most willingly follow the suggestion of the Committee of the Berkshire Bar, and present the resolutions which I have just read. I ask leave also, from my place at the Bar, which I occupied so many pleasant years, in the company of our deceased friend and brother, to speak a few words expressive of kindly and admiring memories of him.

According to the law, and the customs of those times, INCREASE SUMNER was admitted an Attorney in the Court of Common Pleas, in 1825; an Attorney in the Supreme Judicial Court in 1828; and a Counsellor in 1830. Since the latter period, I have known him and his professional life and character. But it was in January, 1834, that we met in Boston as members of the House of Representatives. It was my first and his second year in the House. We took rooms together during that session, and became intimately acquainted. His experience was of essential service to me at that time, as his legal learning and experience have aided me on many occasions since.

As our lives advanced, we became separated in political opinions, and were repeatedly the candidates of the rival parties for the same offices. I was sometimes employed in cases in the courts with him, but more frequently, on the opposing side: and by speech and writing we have had some contests, arousing fully whatever of energy and ability we possessed. Yet, as far as I know, neither in the political field, nor in the courts, have our differences ever wrought any, except merely the temporary estrangement of an hour. I am therefore but doing for him to-day, what I am sure he would have done for me if I had died and he had lived. Alas, the little that I can do—the little that I can reproduce from his ardent and laborious career, so conspicuous in this community for more than forty years!

To understand the professional and personal character of Mr. Sumner, it is necessary, I think, to recall the memory of the members of the Bar of this County, at the time of his entrance into this arena. He came to Great-Barrington to practice law, and he found the professional field there and throughout the County fully occupied. John Whiting and James B. Hyde, at Great-Barrington; Robert F. Barnard, Edward F. Ensign and Parker L. Hall, at Sheffield; Benjamin Sheldon, at New Marlborough; Thomas Twining, at Sandisfield; Lester Filley, at Otis; William Porter, at Lee; Henry W. Dwight, Samuel Jones and Horatio Byington, at Stockbridge; Robbins Kellogg, at West Stockbridge; Henry W. Bishop and George J. Tucker, at Lenox; Henry Hubbard, Calvin Martin, Luther Washburn, Matthias R. Lanckton and Thomas A. Gold, at Pittsfield; Henry Marsh, at Dalton;

Thomas Allen, at Hinsdale; George N. Briggs and Calvin Hubbell, at Lanesborough; Thomas Robinson, Nathan Putnam and Edmund B. Penniman, at Adams; Daniel Noble and Daniel N. Dewey, at Williamstown, were all in legal practice at that time; and I have omitted the names of some who have passed into other avocations, or were then just entering the profession. These gentlemen were in the full possession of the honors and emoluments of the profession in this County, and they had no idea of relinquishing them, except to those who were able to come and take them. Lawyers of eminence also from the river Counties, such as Isaac C. Bates, Charles A. Dewey, and Daniel Wells; and from the adjoining counties in New York, such as Elisha Williams and Ambrose L. Jordan, came sometimes into profitable cases in this County.

Of the members of our Bar at that time, Col. HENRY W. DWIGHT was the leading advocate, a gentleman of great ability at the bar, as in other departments; of most successful management with juries, a man of uncommon eloquence and address; the late Governor BRIGGS, younger, but dividing the honors with Col. Dwight, and with his cotemporary in age, Judge BISHOP, and with Mr. HUBBARD, whose efforts at times seemed quite as successful as any; and with Mr. BYINGTON, afterwards Judge, and Mr. PORTER, not to mention others perhaps equally prominent and successful. Our deceased friend saw the destiny which he was to work out, and its difficulties. He knew that he must proceed without the advantages of a collegiate education. He was not one of the kind who underrate those advantages, nor by any means was he one of the kind who consider the defects of early training to be without a remedy. The prime of life was before him, and he knew it was sufficient for his purposes; and he seemed to know just as well that indomitable will and industry would be required to enable him to secure the share which he wanted—which was the lion's share—in the legal business and popular consideration of the community. His clear perception of the difficulties to be overcome, and his inflexible determination to overcome them, gave the tone and character to his professional life, and secured for him a great professional success. My friend here present, one of the Justices of the Supreme Court (Judge Colt), I think will agree with me when I say, that no member of this Bar, or any other, who met Mr. SUMNER in opposition, could fail to perceive that his case required his closest attention and his best resources.

The delicate and frequently dangerous duty of cross-examination of witnesses was a power in his hands, and usually exercised with marked effect; but I suppose his closing arguments to the jury exhibited Mr. Sumner as a man and as a lawyer, and as a forensic speaker, in the most favorable light. In the preparation and trial of the case, previous to the commencement of his argument, he had thoroughly and unreservedly identified himself with his client and his interests, and had attacked his opponent's case, wherever he could find an assailable point of any kind, preferring to carry the battle, if possible, into the enemy's country. But, when he rose to his argument, he commenced usually with a clear and candid statement of the case and its surroundings; then developed his theory in regard to it, and supported that theory with a combination of cogent reasonings, sparkling wit, and felicity of personal allusion to the parties, witnesses and counsel in the case, which left a favorable, and often powerful impression, upon the jury and the audience.

There was no doubt of his moral integrity under all circumstances, and to those who knew him well, there was as little doubt of the integrity of his intellect. He reasoned correctly from the premises which he assumed. Usually if we admitted his premises we gave him the case, and therefore we directed our opposing strength against the premises which he had seen fit to assume. After questions of law were prepared by reports, or exceptions for the legal Bench, he gave them full examination with the aid of all the books within his reach, and it was after such examination that I have admired his generally correct anticipations of the final decision of the Court. He was then able, as I thought, to lay off the lawyer and put on the judge, and I was not surprised to find in his brief judicial experience, near the close of his life, he evinced admirable qualities in settling questions both of law and of fact.

Mr. SUMNER was always industrious. He filled up all his leisure time. While attending the Legislature, and the Constitutional Convention of 1853, I observed that his mind was constantly active. He remembered history and biography with accuracy, and he read and appreciated poetry, with a taste which became highly cultivated. He was fond of genealogical researches, and remembered their facts with wonderful accuracy.

Whenever it was announced that he was to deliver an address, upon any public occasion, a full and attentive audience was insured. I well recollect his address before the Berkshire Agricultural Society, full of noble sentiments and eloquent passages. Especially do I remember his address, a few years since, before the Berkshire Bible Society. It was a model speech, and certainly left no doubt of his assured faith in evangelical religion.

But, brethren of the Bar, what need of more words? He has left us, and the few remaining men of his generation are soon to leave you. Nearly all those whose names I have recounted are gone. With them have gone the Judges of those Courts, upon whom we used to look as pillars which were never to decay. With them has gone CHARLES SEDGWICK, the all accomplished Clerk of these Courts—whose mind was as clear as his heart was kind—and whose words and letters remain to us.

In response to the request to allow the resolutions to be placed on record, His Honor, Judge Devens, briefly expressed his concurrence in and approval of the ceremony of manifesting the esteem of the Bar for one who had so long filled a large space in the courts and practice in the County. Twenty years ago he had quite intimately known the deceased, who was then District Attorney for the District comprising the four western counties. He knew him as an able advocate, a wise counsellor, and an industrious, honest, courageous member of the profession. His acquaintance and knowledge of Mr. Sumner were such that he knew him to be worthy the eulogies of his brethren, and in respect to the deceased he would adjourn the court.

Judge Colt, Rev. Dr. Todd, and other prominent citizens and professional gentlemen from all parts of the county, were present, and there were other speeches and eulogies ready for delivery, but the adjournment came while the lawyers were modestly waiting, one for another, to pay their respects, and many kindly and good words were left unsaid.

BANQUET OF THE BERKSHIRE BAR.

CORRESPONDENCE.

PITTSFIELD, December 5th, 1870.

BRO. SUMNER:

At the close of the late Court, several members of the bar met and had a very pleasant social meeting. We then resolved to invite a meeting of the Bar, and to have a Bar Dinner at the American House on the 28th inst., and with one accord it was agreed that you should be solicited to preside over the festivities. Your long standing and eminent position at our Bar, induced us with hearty unanimity to solicit your attendance as the pre siding officer of the meeting. There is no reason why we may not have a profitable time, and one that may stimulate us all to emulate and sustain the good reputation which the profession in this County has at all times heretofore sustained. We hope you will favor us with your presence. Enclosed please find a circular which has been prepared and forwarded to the members throughout the County. We address you as a committee of the late meeting, specially authorized. Hoping you will find it convenient to attend, we remain yours, &c., MARSHALL WILCOX,
S. W. BOWERMAN.

GREAT-BARRINGTON, Dec. 10th, 1870.
Hon. Messrs. Wilcox and Bowerman, Committee of the Berkshire Bar :
MY BROTHERS:—The happy thought of having a social gathering of the Bar of this County, and an appropriate festival, as suggested in your kind letter of invitation to me, is exceedingly gratifying, and if I can in any way aid, I shall most cheerfully do so. As well the resident members of the Bar, as also those who have gone out from us, and reside elsewhere, I should hope might be solicited and induced—with other distinguished guests—to attend. In this connection I might recite many honorable names, but will

4

mention one—WILLIAM C. BRYANT. He practiced at our bar, I think, from 1816 to 1825, with distinction and success, and then retired from legal practice, and removed from Massachusetts to occupy his present field of renown. So long as "Monument Mountain" stands, or the "Green River" flows along its beautiful banks, his name in Berkshire will be remembered and honored. Of those who have practiced at our bar, he is, I am quite sure, the eldest survivor. His presence at our proposed meeting is certainly greatly desirable. Aside from those who are, or have been members of our bar, are many who having here finished their preparatory legal studies, left for other sections of our country and have risen to be the pride and ornament of our profession abroad at the Bar, and many of them upon the Judicial seat. Their presence with us would be highly gratifying. And I hope most earnestly, that all the brethren now of our county, will by no means fail of attendance. Collectively speaking, it may well be said of the members of the Berkshire Bar, they need not be afraid or ashamed to have their fellow-citizens look upon them, whether at the bar or the banquet, for they have never wronged their noble profession.

With sentiments of great respect,

Very truly yours,

I. SUMNER.

BANQUET OF THE BERKSHIRE BAR.

The following account of the Banquet of the Berkshire Bar, referred to in the foregoing correspondence, which took place December 27th, 1870, and was the occasion of the last meeting of Judge Sumner with his professional brethren, is taken from the Berkshire Courier of January 11th, 1871 :

" The meeting and festival of the Berkshire Bar, as arranged, took place last week Monday, at the American House, Pittsfield. Before dinner— which was at 5 P. M.,—most of the members of the bar convened and formed an association, one object of which is an annual meeting to be held on the last Wednesday of December. The officers of the association are Judge Sumner of Great Barrington, President; H. J. Bliss, Esq. of Adams, Vice President; and James M. Barker, Esq., of Pittsfield, Secretary. About sixty were at this dinner, including invited guests, amongst whom were Rev. Doctors Todd and Strong of Pittsfield ; Hon. W. G. Bates and District Attorney Gillett, of Westfield ; Doctor Sabin of Williamstown; F. Chamberlin, Esq., of Hartford, and others. The tables were spread with great elegance, and the provision was most sumptuous—nothing seemed to be omitted. The feast at the table being over, the intellectual feast began. Several letters were read from gentlemen unable to give their personal attendance. Judge Sumner made the opening speech. His topic was 'The founders of the Berkshire Bar.' He presented Berkshire as being before 1761, a part of the county of ' Old Hampshire,'—a fact we should ever be proud to hold in remembrance. The Hampshire Bar had existence certainly as soon as 1686. Much irregularity in legal practice in the early days prevailed. People then had crude ideas as to the legal profession or judicial proceedings. Judges, in fact were appointed, not because they were learned in the law, but—so it would seem—because they were NOT learned. Legal learning, instead of being sought was condemned. It almost appeared as though the purpose was to carry suits not in compliance with law, but against it. This state of things continued till past the close of the first quarter of the last century—a new scene was then to open. We are aware that in the formation of institutions from household to kingdom, certain idiosyncracies, capacities, instincts are most surely created, which continue in perhaps endless perpetuity. Hence peculiar family traits are exhibited through successive generations. The traveller of to-day who visits, for instance Germany, hears the same grand old mother tongue which Luther spoke, meets with the same love of poetry and song, and all learning which distinguished that land ages ago. The similar strains of the bag-pipe—the pibroch or war-song—which roused the clansmen of Roderick Dhu, fall yet in grateful cadence upon the Scottish ear. Men pass away, but their successors retain the identity of things as left to them. So in the founding of an institution or association like a law bar; the properties appertaining to its origin may last long after its founders are gone, for their place may be filled and well filled by a long line of successors. Can we not be permitted to say such is the fact in regard to the Berkshire Bar ?

Who, then, were the founders of this bar ? More than one hundred years ago, before our county was formed, a reform of old Hampshire bar occurred, and therefrom as a consequence this bar originated. Phineas Lyman and two of his pupils, viz.: John Worthington and Joseph Hawley were the reformers. Lyman began practice as early as 1743. He was a lawyer of learning and ability, and acquired extensive practice. Worthington was of Springfield, born in 1719, graduated at Yale in 1740, and commenced practice in Springfield in 1744. He was a splendid man, of eminent learning and a finished advocate. By the royal governor of our Massachusetts province, in 1769, the office of Attorney General was tendered to him, but he did not accept. He died in 1800. Hawley was born in Northampton in 1724, graduated at Yale in 1742, and began the practice of law in his native town. He was an able lawyer in all respects, a most worthy man and a distinguished patriot. He was the compeer of the Adamses and Hancock. Judge S. read extracts from a letter of his to John Adams, then in the Continental Congress, written in the fall of 1774, replete with ardent patriotic sentiments. This letter Mr. Adams, on its reception, read to Patrick Henry—it roused him to exclaim with great emphasis: 'I'M OF THAT MAN'S MIND !' Henry's celebrated speech, concluding with 'Give me liberty or give me death,' was made the Spring after. Who can say—said Judge Sumner—but that the inspiring eloquence of that speech may in a measure, at least, have been caused by the inspiring sentiments in Hawley's letter ? In all important trials, Worthington and Hawley were employed. Their great learning, probity and skill taught their fellow-citizens new lessons in regard to legal practice, and the legal profession. Reform was the result. It was a happy memorial of these two

28

men, that old Hampshire caused to be named after them, two of her towns—Hawley and Worthington.

This part of Hampshire—our Berkshire—was then being peopled, and two lawyers of the Hampshire bar, John Ashley and John Huggins, both men of probity, learning and extensive practice, cotemporaries of Worthington and Hawley, settled in Sheffield. Ashley graduated at Yale in 1730, was admitted to the bar in 1732, and died in 1803, at the age of 93. He was largely interested in lands of the lower Housatonic proprietary. They had not the commanding influence at the bar as had Worthington and Hawley, but they were worthy coadjutors with them. They deserve to be named with them as reformers of the Hampshire, and founders of the Berkshire Bar. Our record of Huggins is scanty; we know he was in practice as early as 1743, was skillful, educated and of good repute. The only other lawyer in Berkshire, in 1761, was Mark Hopkins of Great-Barrington, of whose talents and patriotism Judge S. spoke at some length. Pre-eminently did he deserve to be accredited as one of the founders of our bar. He probably read law under Worthington; he was a kinsman of Mrs. W. He advanced in lucrative practice, and into the great confidence and esteem of the community. Withal he was a patriot of the first rank. When the revolution opened—opening as it did in gloom—he laid down his pen, girded on his sword, left the bar and repaired to the field. His position was that of Colonel. He went to White Plains, sickened, and in October 1776, two days before the battle, died. He was the grandfather of the distinguished President, and one of the Professors of Williams College.

Judge S. also alluded to Judge Sedgwick, who studied law under Mark Hopkins, and continued his remarks at length, the foregoing being but an imperfect sketch. Capital speeches were made by Lieutenant-Governor Tucker, Judge Colt, Congressman Dawes, Hon. W. G. Bates, District Attorney Gillette, Henry W. Taft, Rev. Drs. Todd and Strong, Hons. H. L. Sabin and R. Goodman, and others, and a fine poem was delivered by F. O. Sayles, Esq. The proceedings terminated at a late hour. We append the letter of W. C. Bryant, written in answer to an invitation to be present:

" NEW YORK, December 14th, 1870.

" DEAR SIR:—I thank the members of the Berkshire Bar for their kind invitation to be present at their social meeting and dinner on the 28th inst. My nine years of practice at that bar were a useful mental discipline to me, however imperfectly turned to account, and my residence in your beautiful county was a most fortunate event of my life. It would give me pleasure to meet with those who have taken the place of the generation of lawyers to which I belonged, but several engagements require me to remain here and content myself with wishing you all a meeting of which you will long retain a pleasant memory.

" I am sir, very truly and respectfully yours,

" W. C. BRYANT.

" JAMES M. BARKER, Esq., Secretary, &c., &c."

DEDICATION SERVICES.

From the Pittsfield Sun, July 5th, 1871.

DEDICATION OF THE JULIA SUMNER MEMORIAL HALL.

Our readers are aware that at the time of his death, Judge INCREASE SUMNER had nearly completed a handsome four-story brick building in the central block of the village of Great-Barrington, the upper portion of which was designed for a Musical Hall. On his dying bed he said to his eldest son, Samuel—the only child present when the venerable man expired—that the Hall was to be MEMORIAL; to be called "THE JULIA SUMNER HALL," directing that it be dedicated with religious ceremonies. In fulfillment of Judge Sumner's will on the subject, the dedication appointment for the evening of June 28th (last Wednesday evening), was made.

THE HALL

is an elegant assembly room, capable of comfortably seating five hundred persons. The provision for ventilation and heating is abundant, and of the most approved modern contrivance. The experience of the evening demonstrated that the acoustic properties of the place are perfect—both audience and speakers testifying to this main point of excellence in the Hall. Notwithstanding the heat of the evening—which was excessive—the atmosphere was not less fresh and cool in than out of the Hall. The gas lights were of such number and character, and so admirably arranged, that the finest print could be equally well read in any seat. The entrance from the ground is by a flight of stairs leading up the centre of the building; the immediate entrance being by steps from the west end of the second story passage-way, which lead to a mid-way platform, from which, on either hand, the Hall is reached by a half-story flight. At the east end of the Hall, is a platform about three feet high and twelve feet square. On this occasion, immediately in the rear and about eight feet above the platform was suspended a beautiful portrait of Judge SUMNER, painted by the celebrated artist, Mr. Curtis of Bridgeport, Conn. This portrait is an excellent likeness of Judge SUMNER, as he appeared ten years ago—and as we gazed upon the painting, in which the features of the wonderfully handsome old man are depicted with rare artistic skill, we could not do otherwise than recall many a court scene in which *he* bore the prominent part, and in which he manifested a power of logic and of eloquence such as is rarely exhibited in any tribunal of justice. And, furthermore, it occurred to us, that our bar would only be paying a proper testimonial to the memory of such a lawyer, if they procured a copy of this painting and placed it in the new Court House. Beneath the portrait of Judge SUMNER— was a large "touched" photograph of the beloved daughter, "JULIA," after whom the Hall is named.

THE AUDIENCE, AND THE SPEAKERS.

A brief paragraph in the Courier of Wednesday, of the previous week, was the only advertisement we saw of the Memorial Exercises that were to take place; and that simply announced the purpose, and extended a general invitation. It seemed to us that the notice was insufficient, as it certainly was very modest. It was announced that the exercises would commence precisely at 8 o'clock; and as we had been incidentally assured by many persons that there would be "plenty of room" we made no haste "to be there"— arriving at the street door at a quarter to 7. We found the passage-way completely packed with persons anxious to obtain an entrance to the Hall; ushers at the mid stairway landing occasionally shouting down the assurance that they were trying to make as much standing room as possible. We were about taking our departure in a spirit of great disappointment, when the agent in charge of the building, Mr. F. T. Whiting, recognized and seized us, and informed us that an eligible seat had been reserved on our account. We were duly installed in our "reserve," where we had twenty minutes in which to note some of the items already recorded, before the exercises commenced. We should note also that the platform had been temporarily extended on the right of the permanent stage, so as to furnish room for a piano and a large cabinet organ. As we have indicated, the Hall was crowded to excess, it being estimated by the ushers that there were about six hundred persons in the audience—several hundred coming to the street entrance and being obliged to retire, for lack of even standing accommodations. (We have been informed that it is in contemplation to build a horse-shoe gallery at the western end of the Hall—thus affording seats for 150 more persons.) Shortly after we entered the Hall, the noise attendant upon taking seats subsided— as all the seats were occupied, and standing room was not obtainable. The audience silently gazed upon the portraits of the once familiar faces—the father and daughter—the shadows of whose remarkably pleasing countenances looked down upon us (if we may so write) from the centre line of the eastern wall. Precisely at 8 o'clock there was a buzz of announcement: the widow and the three sons of the deceased Judge entered the Hall. Mrs. Sumner is the second wife of the Judge, and the step-mother of "the boys." She took a seat in the third row of settees from the platform, while "the boys"—as we heard every one around us call them—proceeded on and took their places on the platform: Samuel B., of Bridgeport, and Charles A. and

31

Albert I., of San Francisco, California. The Rev. Evarts Scudder, Congregational, the Rev. Dr. Olmstead, Episcopal, and the Rev. Mr. Akerly, the Methodist clergyman of the town, were then invited to occupy assigned places on the stage. At ten minutes past eight the exercises began with an original Voluntary by Prof. Albert I. Sumner. But before we comment upon the exercises, we will give the programme, as follows:

ORDER OF EXERCISES.

1. Voluntary on the Organ—original. Albert I. Sumner.
2. Prayer, by Rev. Evarts Scudder.
3. Requiem—Piano—original. Albert I. Sumner.
4. Introductory remarks. Samuel B. Sumner.
5. Hymn—original. Samuel B. Sumner.
6. Memorial Address. Charles A. Sumner.
7. "Separation"—Piano—original. Albert I. Sumner.
8. Doxology.

The musician of the family, Albert I., has already obtained considerable celebrity as a composer of Organ and Piano Music; and both as a composer and performer we had direct and most pleasing evidence of his ability during the evening. His " *Voluntary*" on the Organ was a fit prelude to the services which were to follow; but it was left for his *Requiem* to develop his positive genius for appropriate musical composition.

The prayer by Rev. Evarts Scudder was a choicely-worded appeal for the Divine blessing upon the family of the deceased, upon the community in which they were again assembled from afar, and upon the meetings that hereafter may be held in the structure they were to dedicate.

The introductory remarks by Samuel B. Sumner were apt and impressive. He briefly recounted the circumstances connected with the planning and erection of the building, and in most affecting tones related the dying father's directions to his " dear boys," as he called them, "concerning the dedication of the Hall." In obedience to the father's express mandate, and in conformity with the inclinations of the sons, no entertainment was to be permitted in the building, at which a young lady of refined and cultivated tastes, like Julia Sumner, might not properly attend—at which *she* might not have laudably desired to be present. Since one of the sons had last taken his departure for his distant home, in California, sister and father had passed away; and it was thought eminently proper that he should give the formal, extended expression to the suggestions and sympathies that pertained to the occasion.

The following Hymn was then sung;—almost the entire audience, apparently, participating in the singing:

HYMN—BY SAMUEL B. SUMNER. *Air—Greenville.*

Now let gentle memory lead us,
  While this hour our thoughts recall
Forms of loved ones who precede us
  Whither we are hastening all;
Weak we know our best endeavor,
  'Gainst the Lethean wave to strive,
Still with human fondness ever,
  Would we keep our dead alive.

His behest this hour obeying,
  Who for sake of memory dear,
Crowned an earnest life, essaying
  These memorial walls to rear;
Thus we gather, while we listen
  To familiar tones of yore,
And while eyes in sadness glisten,
  Here to glisten nevermore!

Side by side they now are sleeping,
  Sire and daughter, in the tomb;
Kindred from afar stand weeping,
  And all hearts are filled with gloom;
She in womanhood's first dawning,
  He of ripe three score and ten,
Both lie waiting that bright morning,
  When God's own shall wake again.

'Neath the flow'rets o'er them blooming—·
  Summer's verdure, winter's snows—
Only Faith our souls illuning,
  We must leave them in repose.
So, wherever God shall call us,
  Wide world o'er, our lines to cast,
And whatever fate befall us,
  Death shall claim us all at last!

Father, sister, our sad pleasure,
  With fraternal, filial care,
This fair cenotaph to treasure,
  So its walls your names shall bear;
And when loved ones gone before us,
  Wave for us their welcome wands,
Each and all, may God restore us,
  To the "House not made with hands."

It is impossible for us to give even a satisfactory sketch of the Memorial
Address, by Charles A. Sumner, which followed the singing of the Hymn.
He commenced at a quarter to 9 o'clock, and concluded at 20 minutes to 11.
It is sufficient compliment to the speaker, undoubtedly, to say that the attention paid was absorbing and almost breathless. The orator at first, by a
few touches, carried his auditors back to the Barrington of forty-five years
ago, and then introduced his father as the attorney successor of William Cullen
Bryant, and the youthful colleague of the renowned Gen. Whiting. He gave
what he termed "glimpses" of the biography and characteristics of the father, illustrating some remarkable peculiarities of the man, with well-au-
thenticated anecdotes—names and localities being given in every instance.
Then referring to the death-bed directions concerning the dedication of the
Hall, the orator passed on to a very entertaining sketch of the life and character of JULIA E. SUMNER—the daughter, of great gifts and accomplishments, whose brilliant "promise," acknowledged by all acquaintances, was,
alas! unfulfilled, because the enemy, Death, prevailed when she was
at the early age of 24 years. The speaker then briefly, but forcibly,
presented what he considered the leading trait of both father and child,
which was most beneficial in the community; and the points in their exam-

ple most worthy of imitation. At one period of his address, he dealt in some caustic illustrations concerning the "*smart* girls of the period"—(of which he averred Julia Sumner was not)—which provoked demonstrations of applause and merriment, despite the known seriousness and solemnity which belonged to the object of the meeting. The address contained many points of philosophical suggestion and reasoning, and it will unquestionably be road with profound interest, if it is published, on account of its personal and its general historical information, and its original deductions concerning character and influence. When the orator retired, the audience could not bo restrained from indulging in long continued applause.

At the close of the address, Mr. Samuel B. Sumner thanked the audience for their attendance and attention; Prof. Albert I. Sumner played his origi-nal and exquisite composition, "SEPARATION," on the Piano: the Doxology was sung, and the audience dismissed with the Benediction, pronounced by Rev. Dr. Olmstead.

We congratulate our neighbors upon the construction of such an elegant Hall in their midst, and upon its dedication in a form and by peculiar and eloquent services, which will long be among the cherished memories of citi-zens of Southern Berkshire.

5

MEMORIAL ADDRESS.

MEMORIAL ADDRESS

CHARLES A. SUMNER,

OF SAN FRANCISCO, CAL.

Forty-five years ago the village of Great-Barrington contained a population of about 400 souls. The old-fashioned, gable roofed houses that stood on either side of the one broad shaded street leading from the bend of the Housatonic, at the southern edge of what is now called Water street to the foot of Mount Peter and onward, all possessed an historic interest; and in the bar-room of the tavern that was situated nearly opposite to this place of assembly, curious stories were nightly told in regard to the British troopers' occupancy of those humble but spacious dwellings. These tales have become traditions—if not regarded as legendary—and only three of the primitive mansions, and they somewhat modernized, remain to speak to us of the verity of those now rarely-repeated records of Revolutionary days.

Forty-five years ago John Quincy Adams was President of the United States, and Levi Lincoln Governor of the Commonwealth of Massachusetts. Forty-five years ago General Whiting, an attorney and counsellor, distinguished not only throughout the County, but the Commonwealth, had his office at the junction of Main and Castle streets, and with clients attending from all portions of the State west of the Connecticut, was absorbed in a large and very profitable practice. William Cullen Bryant was also a lawyer, resident in this village forty-five years ago. Unhappily, disgusted with the verdict against his client in an important suit, he, at the date to which we refer, determined to remove from this place to New York City—there to engage in the more congenial, and as it proved to him, far more lucrative business of superintending the publication of a daily journal. At that date a young man of twenty-four years of age, who had run a "collegiate course of three months"—as he was wont to term it—"in a log school house in Bethlehem;" who had educated himself from that graduation so that he became competent to teach in the country; who with his $8 per month earnings on the farm and in the school-room, aided a little by the contributions and much by the cheering encouragement and counsel of an elder brother, had articled himself to Lester Filley, Esq., of Otis, and devoted five years to the study of the legal standards in that gentleman's library—a few months in each year still being occupied with teaching service in the rural districts,—at that date this young man, having learned of the vacancy about to be created by the departure of Mr. Bryant, and wooed to the selection, it may be, by attractions which were not of a professional character, with only a pine-tree shilling in his pocket, crossed the mountain, and came down into this village, and commenced the practice of law in Great-Barrington. There are, I presume, some persons present who can look back through all this vista of years with uninterrupted vision, and bear testimony, step by step, as the perfect chronicler recites the prominent incidents in the life we are to briefly contemplate to-night. Here and there, to-night, it is our privilege, in response to an undoubted desire on your part and with reverent affection for ourselves, to sketch a scene and dwell upon a characteristic.

All the earliest home cotemporaries of our father tell us that his advent created something of an excitement in the society of our village; and the young man was thoroughly inquired about and looked over by the good people who formed the acknowledged aristocracy of the town. And immediately after his settlement, his abilities, his peculiarities, and the future of which he gave promise, were topics for general gossip. And by and by it became subject of friendly remark that he manifested a decided partiality for an afternoon and twilight walk to the old red house, and a rest under the famous horse chestnut tree that stood in the yard beside the old red house situated on what is now the Dr. Collins' homestead,—then occupied by the widow and children of Dr. Samuel Barstow.

But I do not intend to trespass upon your patience with a biographical record; which would be imperfect, and to many of you suggestive of more interesting points than those presented. Enough to throw your minds back to the year 1825; and more or less, as we are individually able, to realize the time that has passed, the length and breadth of the years that compose the citizenship and professional career in Great-Barrington of Increase Sumner.

It is a long while ago, my friends. The population of the United States was then less than ten millions; there was not a mile of railroad in the country, and it was then more than ten years prior to the invention of the telegraph. And after ten years' absence your children come back to you hardly recognizable, with their added weight of days marked upon their countenances and indicated in their altered voices and sobered mien.

If in this period of time a man that has lived and served in the same village and occupied a prominent position by his works, is not thoroughly understood by his intelligent neighbors, there must be singularities about him which defy the power of human scrutiny. In the crowded city the public servant may be imperfectly known to his most intimate associates; for the opportunities to closely observe even a character that is absolutely free in its development are oftentimes wanting in such a place. There men " touch and go" and leave no certain and full picture on the memory of the nearest acquaintance. In most respects, my friends, the majority of persons before me must have understood the man of whom I am speaking as completely as it is possible for those outside of his family-circle to have comprehended his nature and motives. Therefore, what may be properly said to-night in review of his life will meet with your concurrence from an actual recollection, and be carried out in your minds with illustrations that are all your own. And here the words may be spoken which are fit and proper only in such a presence and on such an occasion ; here these words will not render us amenable to any charge or suspicion of egotism or foolish pride. Let us proceed.

Much of that I am about to say is necessarily and gratefully drawn from the general testimony which many of you have incidentally given long ago, concerning the strength and struggles and triumphs of the man.

There was a quality and habit common to the American youth of those days, of which more is now sung but less practically known. A PERSEVERING INDUSTRY distinguished the life we commemorate, in a remarkable degree. His ambition, which was avowed and ardent, had no fanciful or hap-hazard phases. Confident in his abilities without conceit, he was yet ever most reliant upon the valor and virtue of hard work. When Stephen Cone gave him his first important case he sat down and investigated every point with such an amount of patient toil, and brought forth an argument which evinced such great labor as well as good judgment, that his earliest, prominent patron had to make it known to all his friends that his suit had been gained by a young attorney who omitted nothing that could have the least weight in the trial, but pressed every fact with discriminating zeal ;—who obtained not only the verdict of the jury for his client but evoked the unusual and inadvertent compliment of the judge that instructed the panel. The industry that may be said to have been relentless in its character was exhibited in this man's career ; and he was entitled to encourage his fellow-men—as he often did—with admonitions and appeals in behalf of the dignity of labor, as comparatively few men now are authorized to exhort in this indeed busy but far less earnest-working world of ours. For his profession his preparation was strong, and the fundamental requisite of a disposition and determination for labor was ever-present with the man.

But mere diligence can achieve but little at the best; the measure of success that is notable in the profession named must depend upon the rarer gifts of nature. There may be a prominence in political life obtained through adventitious circumstances or by arts that are mean and discreditable; but the solid respect of the world must be acquired by faithful and unremitting labor in the legal profession, by the man of high mental endowments. The habit of industry may be cultivated to a great extent, and perhaps may be said to be planted in natures originally predisposed to utter slothfulness. But, *power of mental concentration* is a faculty of real genius. Not merely to work all the minutes of an hour and all the working hours of a day, but to labor straight towards an object and for the accomplishment of the purpose first had in view,—this is the cunning of business. There are those who severely bend every energy they have under a resolution to perform certain deeds and secure certain results; and yet they never have a chance to celebrate a considerable victory, because despite their most honest efforts they vary from the true path of labor, they push unwittingly into by-ways, they waste their toil; so that their strength of application is but vanity and their end disappointment. These persons must judiciously confine their aspirations to smaller services, or they will only have constant cause to mourn fruitless periods of well-meant and exhausting struggle.

There is an instinct in zest, in relish, which lightens or obliterates the sense of toil : denoting adequate capacity for given duties and predicting success in them. In itself, by itself, drudgery never began, conducted and completed a great undertaking, or wrought out a creditable biography. There are simple and most familiar acknowledgments of this truth in political matters, in every-day life. And we are prepared to say in all candor, and with your known approval, that conjoined with an iron will for duty there was in

6

Increase Sumner a love for his calling that made his study his delight, and prophesied his days of happy diligence, abounding with professional victories.

In his constitution and character there was among other fundamental elements the sense and faculty of HUMOR; humor in appreciation and expression. As an appropriate part of the man, and as a great possession with him personally, this element was fundamental. A man without humor may grow rich on his shrewdly obtained compound interest; he may give what are termed substantial evidences of his "thrifty manhood;" but he is only just within the pale of humanity, genuine humanity,—that is all.

I have almost forgotten how Seekonk and Alford and Muddy Brook appeared when I last rode through their gates, and I shall probably never see them again; but now and at any time hereafter you and I can people those and many adjacent places with the old inhabitants of twenty and thirty years ago, because we both saw them painted in words of comedy, in an address to the justice here or the jury at the shire town, by Increase Sumner, Attorney and Counsellor at Law. We may see these men again and again, and try to believe that they have grown to be different, because older men; but there the original painting remains. By a sentence or clause uttered in perfect mimicry, or by one singular, all-comprehensive, metaphoric word, enhanced it may be with a gesture, portraits were given by this consummate artist,—frescoed on the gallery walls of every listener's memory,—there to abide forever.

The GOOD TASTE that was a leading feature in his unnumbered arguments, his scores of lectures and his conversation was in great part the result of a special, assiduous cultivation. An innate thirst for the higher literature and its gratification,—it may be insensibly, but as the result of his reading—produced a marked and happy effect upon the style of his discourses, and made his speech a constantly improving exhibition of the neatest, most precise, most entertaining forms of rhetoric. Much has been said of late years by

leading professors in law-schools, and prominent practitioners at the
bar, about the alleged inevitable injuries to the powers for legal
debate consequent upon general "indulgence" in the libraries of
belles-lettres. The character and life on which we meditate contradict this warning,—which I presume some good old dry-as-dust
originated for Authority, and many young law tutors have repeated
out of pure respect to precedent. Here was a young man whose
natural inclination to the studies deprecated was promoted by the
desire to supply what he presumed, (and rightly,) were marked de-
ficiencies in his regular discipline for his calling; and whose addresses before judges and jurors, as well as promiscuous audiences,
give abounding evidences of the great value to him of his late but
extensive roamings in the fields of exalted, miscellaneous literature.
A brief, extemporaneous obituary address delivered by him some
ten years ago was recently shown to one of the most distinguished
journalists in the country, with the request that he should give his
opinion, from the rhetoric, as to its probable author. And without
hesitation, after the reading, the competent critic whose judgment was
invoked, declared that although there were peculiarities about the
address which induced him to believe that it was by an author with
whom he was not acquainted, still he could imagine that the "elegant text" was the composition of Edward Everett.

ENTHUSIASM was a prime, distinguishing element in the character of the man. Its importance in his profession is perhaps no
greater than in many others that may be named, but in no other is it
more decisive in what are known as exigencies of practice. Even
a physician needs enthusiasm; and the preacher requires it absolutely, if he is to convert many. But without it, the lawyer is never a thoroughly successful advocate before a jury. Indeed, every
true man is an enthusiast;—and the woman without enthusiasm
does not rightfully belong to her sex. A man may be industrious,
methodical, with a basis of good judgment, with a fountain of caustic wit, with a gift of language, schooled and learned; but if he
does not possess the rich quality of enthusiasm, he is lamentably

deficient. A man without enthusiasm may excite admiration for himself but not for his cause ; he may himself commiserate, but he cannot beget in others emotions of personal sympathy. His statement of facts may be marvellously clear and skillful, and his logical deductions may be as sharp and exact as the circumstances of the case will allow ; and he may riddle the opposing evidence with spears of quick analysis, contrast, and personal invective. The jury may pity the unfortunate client or witness against whom he turns the cold and bitter stream of satire with merciless art. Here comes the less able but enthusiastic advocate, who takes inspiration from the fears and sufferings and desperate situation of his poor client, whom he believes to be the party wronged or unjustly accused ; and he puts his nervous fellowship into that jury, he inocculates them with his hot heart's blood ; and presently there are twelve men before him, ready and anxious to declare for the rescue of the person whose miseries are portrayed, and if possible to outrun their mesmerizing captain in the service of executing sudden justice upon the complainant who is now arraigned before the bar of justice ! The complaisant attorney is heard and seen with interest and even with awe, as he deals out his pungent blows against the parties whom he would punish by the verdict. The enthusiastic advocate is not a third person at all, but transmits all his opinions, convictions, hopes and resolves into the gaping triers before him ; until twelve men are tormented before the appointed time in which to announce the decision of acquittal.—Join to industry and sound discretion, and humor, and a correct sense of the proprieties, the glow of enthusiasm in the lawyer and advocate ; and while he will gain many suits that are of doubtful value, before an incorrupt tribunal,—in a perfectly good cause, he is glorious and irresistible ! Such a lawyer and advocate was Increase Sumner.

You will pardon me for saying in this connection that the enthusiastic man is always a prominent target for the envious, or the honestly-made assaults of the phlegmatic nature. " O ! He is too fast !" " He is inconsiderate !" " He is devoid of philosophy !" " He has no balance !" "He is a *fool !*" Worse yet : "He has no manners !" The non-enthusiast has a mountain from whence to criticise. See him ! He never sings ; he drawls : he never preaches ; he prates : he never laughs ; he grins : he never cries out ; he sniffles : he never storms ; he sulks : he may never positively offend anybody ; he does disgust a few : if he rarely does anything that comes palpably under the category of grievous wrong, he does not often accomplish much of substantial good : and if he does rob widows and orphans you cannot detect him at the trade. Enthusiasm is Energy, Motion, Progress, Attainment ;—it is Life ;—it is Humanity !

The enthusiastic lawyer, whose thoughts are concentrated upon a case in which his feelings have become deeply interested, is rapidly walking from his house or his office to the court room where the issue is about to be tried. A good man in the Parish, one of the leading church officers, crosses up to his path directly, stops when in front of him and dogmatically exclaims : " It is pleasant weather !" The sun has already been shining six hours of the day, and there is not a babe in any household round-about that does not know that the weather is pleasant. The interruptedly-halted man—(not merely saluted)—replies in the affirmative, in a brusque and indignant tone, and sweeps past and on. The pious neighbor immediately relates the story of the very brief wayside interview, and then carries about a hand-basket of charity with which to sprinkle and cover the recollection of the surly sin. And eulogies will be written in which this offence on the edge of the highway shall be sadly and forgivingly commented upon by the speakers. A little common sense would explain what charity is unnecessarily summoned to excuse ; and a little more common sense in an earlier day would have prevented the provocation which was rightly resented and rebuked.

There is a compensation for labor in the satisfaction of refreshment and rest that follows. The most enjoyable companionship is that of the man industrious in some legitimate calling, whom you

meet in an appointed or accidental interval of leisure. Then the
social qualities, if they exist, are manifested with singular felicity.
So it was with our father and friend. I need not recall many personal scenes; I can make a personal appeal. You remember how
it was on such a day or such an evening, when by some unforseen
circumstances you were thrown into his society, and made mutually
dependent for temporary entertaining. Perhaps it was a new revelation to you of the man, although you had known him, as you
believed, for many years before. How surprised you were to learn of
his acquaintance with your ancestry: and of your later relations, such
a treasury-house of anecdote! And then, of your own life you
had lost, until he revived it, the happy recollection of a scene in
which you figured conspicuously, and concerning which in some
professional manner your companion had ascertained and once employed the facts. What a Town Chronicler! Absolutely free
from the spirit of mere gossip, having no sort of delight in the stories which malice concocts or exaggerates and spreads, but with an
unmitigated scorn and disgust for everything of that kind, he
caught all the important items in the current news; and they were
graven on his wonderful memory of steel. And in relating the
anecdotes that possessed the shades or pith of humor you would
see that he was saturated with the fun, and to his fingers' ends
tickled in every nerve of his nature. O, how he would tell the
story of some neighborhood disagreement: ending in an equity
suit and rounding off with a trial and admonition in the church!

You might be informed for the first time in your life that your
cousin George, on your father's side, married a Doratha Brown,
whose mother was Elizabeth Henry,—and *she* was born on the old
Kilburn farm. "Her brother, your cousin's wife's mother's brother, Ebenezer Henry, was a queer old fellow. He claimed a right
of way for an irrigating and mill-race ditch across the upper edge
of Hiram Pixley's farm,—having purchased from Pixley, and own-
ing on both sides of the original farm. He undertook to commence
digging the ditch. Pixley warned him off. Old man Henry sued

on his covenant for discretionary right-of-way. I brought suit for him. He got his authority: went on with his ditch. I told him to go and get Woodworth to make the survey ; but he wouldn't,—he staked out and dug his own ditch. When he got through he found that the lower end of his ditch was higher than the upper ; and the water took a notion that it wouldn't run up-hill. Everybody round was laughing at the old man. To make it worse Pixley had some fine flowing springs in the northeast corner of his land, and he run a furrow down from them, a distance of about ten rods, and brought the water into this ditch, and used it himself ! Old man Henry couldn't stand that. So he undertook to fill up the ditch. Pixley warned him off from his premises. But the old man persisted. Then Pixley sued Henry for trespass. I brought the suit. Beat him. Got an injunction and damages. The Court held, as we claimed : that while Henry had a right to dig a ditch across the premises he had no right to fill one up ! And he could not dig a new ditch for the time of his covenant for that purpose had lapsed. I guess the ditch is there to this day. It is a good ditch ; if you only turn the water in at the right end. Yes, yes : old man Henry was a brother of your cousin George's wife's mother."

We shall proceed to higher qualities and considerations. Imagination and the Sense of the Sublime, were constantly manifested by the man ; in his patronage, his study, his instructions, his reasonings. Among the earliest purchases, for his private miscellaneous library, were treatises upon the fine arts, and copies of the standard poets as they were then catalogued—the volumes now well-worn—all dated within the first years of his married life. And while he avoided, as he would any species of affectation and pedantry, that cheap habit—possessed and practiced so widely at the present day—of quoting a familiar paragraph from Shakspeare or Milton, whenever possible to assert or assume an application, he could and did in an unexpected, and therefore original mode, not unfrequently drive home the conviction of the truth of an argument or

theory with a most apt and charming verse or sentence from one
of the masters in English classical literature. And woe unto the
fluent adversary, who thinking he had all the knowledge and virtue
of the text on his side, extracted an illustration from a chapter, or
act, or epic, which, in itself or with the aid of adjacent or by the
light of independent, neighboring phrases, of the same author, admitted of a shifting or reversing of the force that was thus brought
to bear. The danger and disaster incident to such a careless deal-
ing with the dramas of Shakespeare, or the books of Milton, or the
stanzas of Bryant, was demonstrated on many a "well-fought field"
at the Berkshire bar; and youthful lawyers became prudentially
advised of the necessity for weighing and meditating on the whole
of the play of King Lear, before they mouthed any of the crazy
monarch's philosophy in their speech to the jury as counsel opposing the veteran graduate of the Bethlehem log school-house. For if
the reading be faulty, the connection mistaken, the point subordi-
nate to some large sentiment, which in its breadth of gravity
weighed the rather to the other side, the response would come; and it
were better that that quotation had not been born.

An extensive reading in general literature, and a right compre-
hension at all times of the real gist and conclusion of the author,
was an important part of this man's character and available store.

In light literature, his range of acquaintance was wide and cotem-
poraneous. Pardon this personal statement : I never saw my father
reading a novel. And yet I never heard the contents, the characters, of a work of fiction which had obtained creditable popularity,
discussed in his presence, without receiving his judgment of the
book, unquestionably founded upon a thorough understanding of
its plot and dialogue. Walter Scott was a familiar favorite with
him; and I remember to have heard him say that the world seemed
to have darkened when he learned of the death of the wonderful
" Wizard of the North."

In treating of the common law doctrines applicable to an important case, he once quoted from the prefatory portion of a novel by

G. P. R. James; and the eminent Judge who decided the case in his favor, repeated the " authority."

His love for painting and sculpture,—respecting which his untutored judgment was acknowledged to be excellent,—is perhaps as notorious as any characteristic of the man. And by essays and every practical expedient within his privilege, he sought to create and extend a similar love and appreciation, while as well by this as other modes constantly deepening his own. " In painting and in music,"—I have heard him say,—"God has certainly given us rich hints of some of the finest glories of the celestial world. By their aid I sometimes feel almost inclined to say that I could place a satisfactory existence for eternity."

And having regard to all that I have recently said, a passing direct mention, at least, must be made of the marvelous endowment of Memory. How often have you heard the Judge upon the bench turn from counsel disputing as to the respective accuracy of their notes of testimony, and ask Increase Sumner, if he chanced to be sitting by, what was his recollection of the language of the witness. And you remember with what entire reliance the answer was received both by the Court and the contending attorneys. And such was his recollection of precedent, and the consequent frequency of convenient reference to him by Judges sitting on the Supreme Bench, that Henry W. Bishop once remarked, that " Sumner had been earning a Judge's half-pay during the last quarter of a century." Of faces, localities, pictures and vocal harmonies his mental impressions were clear for a description in detail, even when the opportunity for seeing and hearing had been incidental and imperfect.

Need I say specially, in such an audience, that our father was a keen appreciator of the noblest rhetoric, both of prose and poetry. His elocution declared this to be a fact of his genius, with unimpeachable emphasis. You remember his readings of the Declaration of Independence, and the occasional odes that were prepared for our local celebrations, and his fervid and impressive oratory, when the announced speaker on any public occasion. The combi-

7

nation of humor and enthusiasm and sublimity rendered him remarkably sensitive to the sweet strains of poesy, and fully alive to the power and perfections of eloquence. If you have heard him read Walter Scott's " Song of Rebecca" :—

> "When Israel, of the Lord beloved,
>   Out from the land of bondage came,
> Her father's God before her moved,
>   An awful cloud of smoke and flame.
> By day, along the astonished lands
>   The cloudy pillar glided slow ;
> By night, Arabia's crimson sands
>   Returned the fiery column's glow ;"—

Or if you have heard him read Burns' " Cotters' Saturday Night ;" or Bryant's " Old Man's Funeral ;" or Longfellow's " Village Blacksmith," then you have a red-letter hour from that entertainment which you will never forget.

But above all and beyond all, he was one of the few who are gifted for the reading of Holy Writ ; one of those designed to reveal Scripture by Scripture—the only commentary that is plain and decided and beautiful : the commentary that alone will be when there are no sects on earth, and all shall see eye to eye,—in the millenium. O, delicious echoes of the far-off days ! Wearied of the preaching and the praying, and even the singing in the church ; more weary of the Sunday-school instruction, and most weary of the enforced perusal of the Sunday-school books, in which hideous wood-cuts represented the pitiless Calvinistic wrath of God to man ; even when we least comprehended the significance of the verse, how rejoiced we were as he took up the old family Bible and commenced to intone the sacred text. Then we heard not the reading of the Scribes and Pharisees, but the voice of one having authority. Then we knew that the beatitudes were not platitudes. Then we heard Paul thundering on Mars hill. Then the most neglected vision of the seer of the isle of Patmos, in all its grandeur and glory, was spread out before us. He was an unsurpassed chanter of the songs of the sweet singer of Israel ; and an interpreter of the Book of Job, by nature.

The Rev. Mr. Dale, an eloquent Methodist clergyman, who in the year 1866 preached at Virginia City, Nevada—and who at the time referred to was an entire stranger to me—on one winter's Sunday morning, in the year named, in the course of a sermon devoted to urging the laymen of the congregation to aid in the proselyting service of the parish, took occasion to state that he dated his conversion, so near as he was able to establish such a point in his life, at an hour when he heard—as by accident—a printed discourse by Dr. Melville of England, read in a remarkably clear and attractive manner by a lawyer, in an old stone, Episcopal church, in the village of Great-Barrington, Massachusetts.

Do we not now naturally arrive at the grand, culminating, crowning characteristic of the man ?

O, brother ! as we sat together in silence by the shores of yonder sounding sea, in that far-off borderland of our Continent, smitten with the tidings of his death, how inexpressibly consoling, how changed the sorrow to mournful but undoubted, animating joy, as we read that one little sentence in the midst of the first testimonial of respect—seemingly considered so unnecessary in the community where he dwelt that it had almost not been said—extemporised by brethren of the bar in the Court over which he but recently presided : " His integrity was never questioned ! " " His integrity was never questioned !". Not: " was always vindicated," or " ever maintained." " Never questioned ! " In a profession, up the gradations of which he struggled from the lowest round in the ladder.; where there is confessedly such a multitude of temptations to commit for temporary advantage's sake, and with slight chance of exposure, the smaller sins of a sharp practice—giving rise at least to a shade of distrust, and warrant by the whispered taunt of the foe,— in a profession where he necessarily provoked hundreds of not overscrupulous persons into keen and lasting enmity—forty-five years in that profession ;—and he never boasting, and no man in his lifetime extolling his integrity : because it never occurred to any acquaintance to dream of suspecting the honesty of Increase Sumner.

And whoever doubted his sincerity of judgment ? Put two ways before him, of right and of wrong, and who of his acquaintance does not know which one he would instantly, and as it were involuntarily, adopt and pursue ?

My friends : I do not despise, I respect his religious connections. But I care little about the accidental machinery of his ecclesiastical experience. We have an Example. I have come up out of the deeps of that bereavement—from the anguish of the blow, from kneeling beside that old man's grave, where he sleeps, where there is no knowledge, or device, or labor, and into which I had always thought I should precede him,—I have come assured anew that the good shall be immortal, and the good alone. Tell me no more that the Universe, or any portion of it, has been or ever will be districted off for the perpetual jurisdiction of police courts, or the everlasting maintenance of county jails. I have seen a life which in respect to one point of heavenly fellowship, is by the plummet perfect:—as the commandment presumed it was possible to be. Faults there may have been abundant. But it requires a creed against the Scriptures to deny the sufficiency of an atonement plead to cover the frailty which belonged to such a man. Seek no more to file off the asperities of my individual humanity, with the raised letters of cast-iron articles of belief—newest brought from the pattern foundries of theology. He that doeth right, and resteth upon Him that was altogether the perfect man, shall live. And the abominations shall be cut off. And the intention is the exclusive centre of inquiry and judgment. I know I speak from the readings and conversations of the man who appointed these ceremonies. He recognized infirmities ; he repented of errors ; he rested in righteous faith and work. Hypocrisy everywhere and anywhere was the test and termination of his most active abhorrence. Shrive no souls for him either with the fragrance of the incense flung from within the chancel from golden censors, and rolled up against the face of the magnificent marble altar of the cathedral. Shrive no souls for him with the pungent aroma of the caraway-seed, that floods and per-

53

meates every country meeting-house in New England. No raiment
or aroma, of human patching, would be accepted by him as the
clothing of Christianity. A text of Scripture torn from its setting
and poked into the crevice of a boulder, did not sanctify the rock
for him as the corner-stone of the true church. Such men do not
become near-sighted and cross-eyed from daily readings and re-
readings of decalogue, and canons, and " land marks," for they
behold, riding on the arch of the rainbow, the promised metropolis
from Heaven, as on the morning of summer storms the sun bursts
through the heavy clouds ;—and they could not do the forbidden
deeds. The tomes of learning and philosophy, so called, which
pertain to discursive, speculative opinions of mankind about the
details of the hereafter, would not be trodden under foot by him ;
but he would walk around them until he could meet, and solicit the
grasp of the hand of the brother alone capable of helping him, because
the saluted friend put as good fruit in the bottom of the basket as
was displayed in the upper rows. And is such a man to lose his
place in the kingdom, because when wearied with over-work he
was irritable and petulant ? Those who participate in rearing such
barriers, who make such tests with accompanying, congenial excus-
es, who devise theologies that would prevent the heavenly ingress
of such a man as we have contemplated to-night, may be accepted
as worthy to form theories for the groove-educated and unthinking
masses ; but they could not be made of any use in a pin-factory.

O ! I have seen a life that shall be restored at the resurrection
morn ! For truth and Christian confidence were his. Take out,
if you will, of the common heritage of this people, his long, brilliant
record in the intellectual tournaments at the Berkshire bar: but,
O, father ! for the constant mirror of thy stainless honor, and the
inspiration of thy righteous, undaunted will : that at the great day
of gathering, and in the Beautiful City, we may all be there !

My friends : we have only taken a glimpse at this character.
And has any word been spoken not borne out, as was indicated, by
the attending, upspringing testimony of the listeners who knew the

man ? If these Points of Personal record, which at first seemed to
be something considerable and egotistic, diminish continually before
your reviving memories—if these hints, fortunately, refresh and con-
nect your personal recollections—then there is the license and warrant to inquire : What was the life-work of the citizen who planned
these foundations ?

It is difficult to arrive at, or even approach a full estimate of the
accomplished mission of such a laborer. If the stranger concedes
the truth of the sketch that has been made with faltering hand, he
must behold from the mere naming of the attributes, a neighbor
and servant in this community, whose influence for good could not
have been other than intense and powerful. Forty-five years' devotion to his profession in Great-Barrington ! Let those whose
memories go back one-third of that period of time, and from that
measurement up to its full compass, recall and reflect upon that
panorama of the past. Take out of the unrolled canvas the form
and figure of that man. From public convocations, from the demonstrated wisdom of public counsels, from the decision of public
issues, take out what you know belonged to his presence and his
efforts, and then seek to realize the loss that has been sustained according to your remembrance. If you lay hold of the wires
attached to an active galvanic battery, you will feel the shock
despite any former disbelief in its electric force ; if you come within
the pulse-circle of a community whose life is largely affected by a
single earnest purpose, you will have to confess the source that
imparts the most strength to the throbbings.

But it may be that so near the power and so familiar with its
contributions, you do not comprehend its magnitude, its vehemence
and accomplishment. So useful, so necessary, it is difficult to accept the fact of his death. Perhaps it is a little matter that first
breaks in upon you the true conception of the vacancy. It may be
a suit at law,—very likely : it may be a town meeting. It may be
interested regret : something you yourself wanted done, of that description which you were wont to lay before him for performance.

It may be, for any one of you, that there is something taking place, or about to take place, advertised, in which you would naturally place him as the 'prominent actor. He is gone! In some such way, the departure of a great man is first truly recognized in the minds of friends and acquaintances who are not of the family household. There is not the affliction that kinship begets; but the impression made in the brain and heart by the action of the man, in the many days that are passed, leaves a seal that is not sensibly effaced, until the blow of some exigency startles one with the sense of actual and irretrievable bereavement. But from the moment there is an awakened realization of the loss, the knowledge of the greatness of the void will grow until the reckoning and the eulogy are complete :—each friend and neighbor for himself. And the estimate will not then be obscured or belittled by the fact that the person mourned did not attain—because he did not seek—political prominence or notoriety.

You cannot compute the life-work by statistics. If you should figure up every act in every Court and every manuscript in every suit, and boast of a given, specific number of cases, and in a large proportion of which there were forensic triumphs, you would feel conscious, after all, of a barren calendar. Such tables would give but a skeleton sketch of the professional labor of the lawyer. An entire, distinct and graphic report of a single important trial in which he fought and won, were worth more as a type-history than the mere diary of his practice—though that would recite enormous annals of industry. And yet it may be stated, properly enough, that the record shows that Increase Sumner performed a greater amount of office labor than any other brother advocate in the same County, during his term of years.

We are proud in being able to point to tributes which his conscientious and scrupulous professional brethren have paid to his public character and conduct. Coming from the leading men of the Berkshire bar, and endorsed by the entire profession in the County, they engrave an eulogy of the highest standard, and give a biographical epitome which will never be challenged. A similar complimentary sketch coming from other circles of the profession, in other States of the Republic, might be received with suspicion, and by a stranger would at best be regarded with indifference. But the saying and the seal of the Berkshire bar, in acknowledgment of the genius and leadership in Increase Sumner, is a genuine proclamation of excellence.

I would only desire in this connection to introduce the testimony volunteered by a former student in the office of our father—now one of the most distinguished judges, on the Pacific coast. I refer to Judge A. C. Niles, of Nevada City, California. Under date of the 23d of last February, he wrote : " Your father did me great service in judiciously directing my legal studies in the right path. He did me a favor once which was in a special sense personal ; but I do not owe him as much for that as for the privilege of studying with one of those men who make our profession honorable. I looked upon your father then, as I do now, as my ideal of a lawyer—I mean a lawyer in the highest sense of that much abused word."

Blessed with a hearty, robust physical constitution—the joint result of inheritance and healthful exercise in his youth—he could answer a share of application which would have broken the majority of men at half his professional years. He pursued his labors during his half century with almost unimpaired vigor. His chosen field was limited. Such a man does not occur many times in a full century ; and in such narrow boundaries, few of his stamp and capabilities are confined. Not that the scope was too narrow for honorable endeavor ; but, evidently, undoubtedly, it might have been broader, with corresponding gain. Loving the village where he wooed and won the mother of his children, bound to the place where his dear ones lay sleeping, he preserved, he maintained his good word and work here ; combining the favor of all those around about who could employ him to vindicate their cause in the Courts of justice ; reaping a generous prosperity from the toil ; and then dedi-cating a portion of his well-earned, and frugally but not stintingly saved revenues, to the construction of the edifice in which you are seated to-night.

His interest and influence in all public local affairs were declared and hearty. For years and years, when it was known that the positions were an extraordinary tax upon his time and energy, he served in places of trust and power, in behalf of his immediate neighbors. And whenever at home or abroad, in the County, or at the seat of power in the Commonwealth, special objects of desire were entertained on the part of our citizens, he was put forward to champion or solicit. Nor on such occasions were his efforts ever lacking or unsuccessful. And you remember what an earnest advocate he was of every proper local improvement; how zealous for the construction and maintenance of good roads, highways for the people between adjacent neighborhoods,—this anxiety and corresponding exertion being of very considerable value to the people before the days of the iron-horse. And for schools, and academies, and cemeteries, and agricultural societies, and fire companies, and town clocks, and every convenience and accessory and adornment of civilized community life, he was ready in suggestion, in counsel, and in ever generous pecuniary support.

His record in the Legislature and in the Constitutional Convention, and in the office of State Attorney, and lastly in the chair of the Judge, exhibited his fitness for promotion to the highest post of civil distinction,—to seats of honor to which he might undoubtedly have attained had he not, of his own choice, almost exclusively restricted his ambition within the bounds of his professional calling.

That there is a remarkable Providence exhibited in his final personal work, for the general good, there can be no question. With a reasonable prospect of ten or fifteen years more of life before he should be called to take his place in the silent chamber, towards which we are all hastening, he rose from his bed one December morning, in 1870, and suddenly exclaimed: " Oh, why am I stricken with such cold and pain ! " He staggered back to that couch from which he was never more to move without the aid of friendly

8

hands, and on which he was soon to breathe his last. He hoped
and expected to have himself stood here to-night and given personal welcome, in the edifice begun in an old but far from decrepid
age, with the plan of a memento for his favorite child. Yet the
work was so far advanced that he had no solicitude about its com-
pletion. " It is all arranged : it is to be a memorial hall ; it is to
be called the Julia Sumner Hall." It would in any event have
been a memorial for himself ; but now it is to be so regarded in a
singularly solemn manner. The appropriateness, the catholicity of
the plan is worthy of your attention and recollection. Not a chap-
el with its restrictions for service, not a costly window of stained
glass in the walls of the handsome church, but a **Free Hall** for the
people, situated in the most eligible block in the town : commo-
dious, well-lighted, well-ventilated, in every respect thoroughly
adapted for all the purposes which its secular, liberty-cheering name
suggests,—A Public Hall. And it is to be called by her name :
" Julia Sumner."

Was she worthy of this honor ? Was it the foolish fondness of
the father, whose pride and partiality in her were not, and ought not
to have been shared outside of the family, that is signified in the
christening of this public chamber ? Who was Julia Sumner ?
Are you called upon, simply out of respect to the memory of the
builder, to name this place as he told his oldest son he desired it
should be baptized ! Or, are we to follow the only will of the deceased father in this respect with indifference, because there is
nothing, in or out of the commonly accepted proprieties which
should make us attach a larger importance to it ! It becomes a
question. For we all know and say that in every cemetery there
are shafts of marble and granite, that have cost more money than
those who slumber beneath them ever gave either in charity or
risked in enterprise, or could be represented as worthy of from any
moral advantage to the world. Then, who was Julia Sumner ? Of
course, many persons who knew the father well did not know the
child. And a very brief reference to her biography will be permit-

ted, as due to the occasion, and valuable in the private record that is to be published.

Julia Elizabeth Sumner, the sixth child of Increase and Pluma A. Sumner, was born on the 20th of October, 1839. She had no sister companions, and her own mother died in the year 1847. Her ample educational facilities were improved with a zeal that elicited the cordial approbation of teachers, and school-girls whom she aided; the testimonials from the latter to her family being among the singular and most affecting portions of the record volunteered on her behalf after she had fallen asleep.

But it was not her scholarship that attracted the larger attention for her, or distinguished her with any great degree of prominence above her youthful associates and friends. She was the full heir to the intellectual vigor of the father, with all the queenly grace and bewitching loquacity of the mother. I am aware that the listener who had no acquaintance to which I make reference in this description, will smile at this apparent fulsomeness of eulogy; but I know I speak to those and to many who could add stronger paragraphs than I shall dare to pronounce, in honest recognition of the accomplishments, and merits, and fascinations of this daughter, and then express regret at the insufficiency of their tribute to the memory of Julia Sumner. It was the fact that her's were the glorious gifts of genius, which in woman defy analysis in their finest touches; charming where she would, and dismissing unpleasant subjects and persons with a royal notice,—in the last decided to the verge of severity, yet after all leaving the impression of a gentle goodnight.

Commencing towards the end of her seminary days to taste the pleasure of the higher magazine literature, she rapidly became enamored with the productions of the best writers our country has produced; and her original criticisms upon the latest review, article or poem by one of the standards, was well worth the trouble and labor of a regular weekly correspondence. And this from a a girl who had not yet reached the twentieth year of her age.

But she never appreciated herself, nor, with a few exceptions, was she in any sense widely appreciated, as a person of remarkable mental powers and womanly blandishments, until there was what may be termed an accidental discovery. For some literary purpose, in addition to those immediately involved, in 1860 a dramatic entertainment was projected and rehearsed in this village : Bulwer's popular play of the Lady of Lyons being the selected piece, and Julia Sumner being cast in the part of the haughty Pauline. The scope which the character affords for the exhibition of dramatic faculties, is familiar to the majority of those present ; and the fact that Julia displayed on the occasion referred to, powers of pathos and general emotional declamation, worthy of the best actresses upon the Metropolitan boards, is well attested by scores of thoroughly qualified judges. However our thoughts may run on the general propriety and character of the theatrical profession, it is a prerogative to say that there was then manifested an ability to take a front rank in a calling which demands the very highest class of talent, in order to obtain any respectable measure of success. Although this was the first and last indication and demonstration of the kind, it was ample for the establishment of a new reputation for our sister ; one which made her sought after by many who had been slight acquaintances, who subsequently learned to love her for a thousand personal attractions of manner and of speech. The element of confidence in herself was roused to new and more appropriate activity, by this success on the little local stage ; and her development in mind was very rapid from that hour.

Her accomplishments, her conversational grace and her literary productions had perhaps nothing of a characteristic precocity about them ; but they were extraordinary as the performance of such maturity as her years fairly indicated. There were a strength and depth of mind which imposed respect, rather than dazzled the stranger or the friend. There was evidence of a thorough and large growth : and promise of glorious things for the future. Had Julia Sumner lived for a score of years beyond her allotted time, she would have

made a name that would have been cherished, not only by her imme
diate friends, but would have been inscribed in the national literary
biographical annals, and the catalogue of those eminent in works
of benevolence and charity. We were just beginning to understand what a genius was unfolding in Julia, and to plan for her the
widest opportunities, when the force of a long smothered malady
focalized, and brought her to the tomb. She herself had her "Mission" selected, and for it she was willing and determined to make
full preparation before she attempted any services in her chosen
field. Meanwhile the principles, the underlying maxim and rules
of the medical profession and the school she proposed to enter, were
heartily accepted and endorsed by her, and she was ready and zealous with her reasons for the faith that was in her. Her nature it
was to pour all her thoughts and energies where her faith directed.
She burned to be about her special business, in the "Mission,"
which she believed had been appointed for her by the Master. Her
earnestness knew none of the chilling limitations which cramp the
half-hearted, though it may be, excellent people who are less acutely
organized. If not everything in her work, then nothing. And you
take such a nature, with its massive brain, with that clear, all-com-
prehending vision, that most expressive face, that pauseless womanly
anxiety for amiable discussion, and devotion unwearied in the cause
she espoused, and set it in any community, and it must swing out
its influence to the world, and bring to bear a power whose results
time could not efface.

Companion girls, now in matronly life ; some of you know what
magnetism and what strength there were in Julia Sumner. In any
civilized and refined circle, it were better to have her for a friend
than an army with banners. I do not fear a failure in the appeal to
personal recollection on her behalf, and in more than justification of
this christening ceremonial. There is not a lady here, who has frequently come within the radius of Julia's intimacy, I repeat, who
could not furnish tokens of a time when she intuitively reached and
revealed their opinions and ideas, and lent some aid and solution to

difficulties which were admitted; sometimes lighting up the whole horizon with the word of explanation or advice. She was ever ready to give out of her store of information and vigorous sympathy. There was not enough selfishness in her nature for use in the domain of physical self-protection. She may be said to have loved to learn of individual trials that were within her scope of relief. Since suffering with offences must come, it was a real pleasure to her to act the physician : witnessing the pain or perplexity with the average of experienced sorrow, but beholding the recovery or the re-coloring, or the illuminating, with rapturous emotions and congratulations of joy. Thus did she show in advance, rather in a spiritual way, that she was eminently fitted for the "Mission" she had vowed to undertake.

Her's should be described rather as a generous than as a merely affectionate nature. Her esteem was fixed upon the abstract and impressional things of life and literature ; her love and anxiety were concerning those matters with which she could so relate herself that she might go about doing good. And there was nothing mawkish in her temperament. And this was because of her inborn passion and delight to renew, reinstate, promote, perfect that which was lacking. She exhibited this in her modes and manner of instruction—engaged as she was in the work of teaching for many years. And the marked success of her labor as an instructress, was undoubtedly due in great part to these natural qualifications. So it was in her own self-examination and self-training work ; so obviously to all in her outward service.

You put that which we term masculine acuteness into the mental and moral organization of some women, and because of the narowness of their heads, you have to take out some of the essential womanly. And then you have a crank, smart woman ; and in order that there may be daily supplication for deliverance from such, let the litany be amended. Ah, but when there is great breadth of crown, and the shrewdness is superadded to the gentleness : blessed are they who live in the society or dwell in the sunshine of such.

The *smart* girl of the period! She will astound; bewitch; tantalize! She may do you some good, young man, perhaps, by rejecting finally the homage you pay in an instant of foolish admiration. She will sing to you that she may sting you with a barbed retort, that comes in answer to the very suggestion that she herself drew from your lips. The smart girl of the period! I have seen her. I will tell you what she is like. She is like one of those Medusas, commonly called by the sailors, "Portuguese Man-of-War;" of which you may have read a description, and specimens of which you may perhaps have seen. They are found plentifully off the south-western coast of South America, and one species abounds on the coast of Florida. Often have I watched them: riding so gracefully upon the waves. There they float upon the ocean billows,—dancing over the surface, as the smart girl of the period sweeps along on the waves of society. And the unsophisticated young man involuntarily brushes back his hair and adjusts his eye-glasses, and looks again, as the phenomenon glides by. O, how charming! How jauntily the fascinating creature rides on the yeasty wave. There she is, with a gauze-flounce covered crinoline, all blown out around her: so beautiful! And there is her fragile, fairy-like body, dressed in a vari-colored waistcoat; her pretty little head and face, with a delicate saucer bonnet on the top of the head; a great chignon protruding behind; over the temples dripping the golden or auburn ringlets; with a score of long ribbons fastened around the neck and streaming in the wind,—these giving no hint of the fang at the end of each one of them, and the force of a dozen Leyden jars of electricity, communicable at any point! O, how charming! And the young man puts his hands slowly down upon the creature. "Ah!" "ah!"—"It will not occur again!" he protests, as maddened with the agony he snaps his crippled fingers. But he will come again. He will renew and cultivate the acquaintance,—judiciously. He will come again, to gratify himself by witnessing a repetition of the little tragedy,—seeing her attract, and charm, and then lance—somebody else!

Such a girl was not Julia Sumner. She was too sensible, too dignified, too highly embued with a sense of the moral power and prerogative of woman. She could not be cruel either to women, men or animals. Some might have deemed her cold; but she always had the true honor of womanhood in her social relations. Her reprimand was candor; her more frequent approbation and cheer were stimulating for all good. And now, my friends, you are counting yourselves fortunate as you remember more and more what she said and did for you and your's; and you are more and more satisfied that her aim and object in life were replete with instructions of truth and mercy. So she was not a smart girl of the period.

Her religious experience was a matter of normal growth; deep and strong. It became more and more independent. And she was indeed precocious in the ascertaining that the place to find a satisfying portion is in the Book itself; leaving the notes of the learned commentator where for the longer interval they belong—on the shelves,—useful only for occasional and very brief reference. And this is not to disparage the work of criticism, but to discourage by the example, the habit of absolute reliance upon the searching and suggestions of others. She built right up from the New Testament, and the Songs and Proverbs and Prophecies : resting on that concentrating and condensing word,—" Thou shalt love the Lord thy God with all thy heart, and thy neighbor as thyself."

Morning and night Julia Sumner could have been found with the New Testament in her hand and an abridged Concordance; di recting to the given subject in an argumentative way. And every day she brought out from the store-house things new and old.

She could tell you that which you had supposed you had learned and understood years before. And yet it would be a fresh communication, and given with such peculiar vivacity, in that bright, quick, sparkling emphasis, that your former recollections were supplanted forever by the new recital. She always described from a tangent : comparison ; contrast ; similitude ; improvements. So in ordinary things. The person just passed resembled a friend in this, and would have been very like another if such a change had been made in her face. The landscape before us will suggest to her the view we had from June Mountain, during the month previous; this flowing stream needs but a slightly deeper hue to be the twin of our own Green River. And it was always so, and always accurate. With many, the reverting thought is now and then indulged or cultivated. With her, always. She was forever setting up her present and comparing it with the past, and suggesting differences: a vision,—a book,—an audience. Instantly would she institute parallels that seemed more and more perfect, the longer they were held in the testing mind to which they were submitted. Beyond these she made her original combinations in connection with the objects examined; often from the hint of a face or part of a landscape, she would commence and outline a picture that would appear clear to the listener as the literal sight. So from the apparently trifling or incidental passage of the chosen author, she would construct an argument that would lead to an entirely different if not opposite logical conclusion.

But to know with confidence how those verses of the Bible, that were commonly acknowledged to have a contrary meaning on their surface, could be reconciled, harmonized, or balanced,—this was her great inquiry. And if you could help her in this, or if she could enlighten you in turn, happy was she for the day; nor would she let you go from such a conference until she had expressly said that she was pleased with the interview, and anxious for a renewed or similar investigation. Like her father,—whom we have heard repeat a thousand times Walter Scott's death-bed saying, "There is no book like the Bible,"—she regarded the Bible as a revelation to be directly, diligently searched; each one for himself or herself. Hers was not a morbid desire to re-examine many times some obscure line or immaterial passage, on which there were abundant opinions; not to scrutinize such passages over and over again until they were ground into tasteless pulp; but a new section for a

9

new day, and the life from the texts as they were shown in their true juxtaposition, to point a moral and support a hope. So the whole book was to be seen as the whole Heavens : enlarging the mind with holy thoughts, and overflowing the heart with emotions of repentance, reverence and love. O ! that she could have lived to have preached both orally and by her publications ! Alas ! that it was not so to be !

On the ninth of October, 1864, she died.

It will be ten years, on the 17th of next month, since I parted with Julia. We were standing on the platform in front of the building that then occupied the ground over which we are now assembled. I am now directly above the spot where we clasped hands for the last time, and where I uttered the last " Good-by." Ten years have rolled away, and the brothers are here once more : all together again in our native valley.

> " I hear the blackbird in the corn,
>   The locust in the haying,
> And like the fabled hunter's horn,
>   Old tunes my heart is playing."

" Good-by, Julia ! " But she did not answer, " Good-by." We unclasped our hands, and she walked a few yards away. And then she half turned round and looked at me,—a farewell look : despondently sad, as though it bore the burden of a premonition. Our eyes met for the moment, during which we both remembered, as persons in some great peril, and travelled the scroll up to days of early childhood. Then she slowly turned her head away and passed with tarrying steps towards home.

Good people : for six years I have tried to realize that your cherished friend and my sister is dead. I have even coldly thought that I ought to feel a more terrible woe in my heart, as a right fraternal tribute for her loss, and that because I did not constantly suffer that experience, there must be some mistake in the message I had received. I believe some of you could corroborate this, with something from your own experience. When I would nearly approach a complete realizing belief in the letters that told of her sickness and dying and burial, I saw those eyes turn upon me as she stood in the middle of the sidewalk beneath us. A frivolous character, a spiritually uninspired woman could not leave that lasting signet of love with any one. I know I shall see her standing there when I go down those steps to-night : and I shall murmur, " Good-by ;" and she will slowly walk away.

You remember how she looked in her life-time, at the instant when she last spoke to you ; for some have written and more have told us that such was the fact. And I note this here, not needed to make an exhibition of feeling, but to properly magnify the appreciation of her gifts. She was indeed of that countenance which " speaks volumes," and seals the thoughts of the mind in the hearts of all acquaintances. Styles and tones of speech can be copied by the trained imitator ; but vain is the art that attempts to transmit a full sentence of joy or sorrow, with an abiding force, by the poetry of the features. There is no possible, successful mimicry in this. And absolutely untrammelled by superstition, knowing now as definitely as I realize my own existence, that she has returned to dust, and her breath to the God that gave it, I dare to intrude this testimony, at this day, to the wonderful mesmeric will thrown into the face of her whose shadow looks down upon us from these walls to night,—exhibited and planted when there was no terror, and when on my part there was no dread lest we should never meet on this unrenewed earth again.

> " Our young and gentle friend, whose smile
> Made brighter summer hours,
> Amid the frosts of Autumn time,
> Has left us with the flowers.
>
> The light of her young life went down,
> As sinks behind the hill,
> The glory of the setting star :
> Clear, suddenly and still.
>
> As pure and sweet, her fair brow seemed
> Eternal as the sky ;

And like the brook's low song her voice,—
A sound which could not die.

The blessing of her quiet life
Fell on us like the dew,
And good thoughts, where her footsteps pressed,
Like fairy blossoms grew.

Sweet promptings unto kindest deeds
Were in her very look ;
We read her face as one who reads
A true and holy book,—

The measure of a blessed hymn,
To which our hearts could move,
The breathing of an inward psalm—
A canticle of love.

There seems a shadow on the day
Her smile no longer cheers ;
A dimness on the stars of night,
Like eyes that look through tears.

Alone unto our Father's will
One thought has reconciled :
That He whose love exceedeth ours,
Will yet take home his child.

Still let her mild rebuking stand
Between us and the wrong,
And her dear memory serve to make
Our faith in goodness strong.

And grant that she who trembling here,
Distrusted all her powers,
May welcome in that holier home,
The well-belov'd of ours."

If Julia Sumner could have been called upon to name the memorial which an affectionate father should determine to construct, we
may readily believe she would immediately, and without suggesting
aid, have planned a public hall like the one in which we are now
gathered. I do not know, but I presume its fitness as an undoubted response to what she would have named, was prominently in the
mind of the builder from the first moment of its conception.
Certainly nothing could be more in consonance with her general
sentiment ; more agreeable to her taste, sympathy and ambition.

But there was a special hour of Dedication. When reared and roofed, and altogether finished in its outlines, the old man,—almost seventy years of age—was stricken down on his death-bed. And in the short interval of fully reviving powers of thought and speech, to his only attending and elder son he formally disclosed his purpose, and solemnly pronounced the dedicatorial words already quoted : " It is fixed; it is to be a Memorial Hall ; it is to be called the Julia Sumner Hall." And with respect to the building, no other direction was given than that which is contained in these three short sentences of baptism. It was enough.

And now, my friends, I ask your indulgence for a few moments more, while I briefly submit some thoughts touching that which I conceive to be the quality and characteristic of both these persons, who are commemorated in this central edifice, which should be held prominently up for approval and example. Our recollections will be distinct and various, as were our relations to the deceased ; and we will yield a certain prominence to the mementoes of thought or deed, which are with us personal,—the keepsakes which one valuable life always bequeaths to surviving companions. But for ourselves, and for such as may hereafter become interested in these lives, we plead the special object for contemplation and study and pattern. What was this quality or characteristic ? It was *an honest self-assertion.* In my mind this is the grand theme which is exemplified—so to speak—and commended with great emphasis in the biography of this father and child. This was the energizing quality, held in conjunction with the strong mental and moral faculties which we have imperfectly indicated. You will not misapprehend. There is an overabundance of brazen-faced impudence in this sin-cursed nation, for which, and in the midst of which, and by its very strength, its possessors foolishly bid decent people to do obeisance to their brawling bravery ; neither good sense nor courage being educated portions of the nature of such " champions." Honest self-assertion, guarded by the sound judgment that almost invariably attends remarkable mental and emotional faculties : of

this I speak. You may call it the courage of conscience ; we want
to get at the element.

Right principles, progressive ideas, without might and disposition
to proclaim and to insist, and to rebut opposing doctrines, and without a frankly admitted enjoyment of the recompense of reward in a
victory—this latter being a mighty stimulant—are of but little use.
A man of intellectual ability and pecuniary wealth, who listens to
and accepts the advice of the wise ones with whom Satan beleaguers
every community, and keep quiet, here and there, as to the truth or
the justice which he knows and feels, when justice should be vindicated and truth spoken, will very likely become immensely popular; he will be pointed out as the example for the young ; and by
his wicked inaction and silence he will do yeoman service for the
master of evil.   There will always be policy comrades raised up to
tell such a man when it is "safe" to speak out and make a loud
voice with timbrel and shawm.   O ! when there are so many to cry
" Amen," and " Amen," and " Amen," refreshing it is to meet with
those who will stand up in the midst of the babbling chorus and object,
and deny, and refute, and reverse.   And it matters not whether this
quality of honest self-assertion be displayed in a larger or smaller
circle of humanity : the satisfaction of every person capable of ap-
preciating the Right is equally intense, when the demonstration
breaks up cliques and overthrows rings, and works out the simple
proprieties.   It is not discontent ; it is not a litigous disposition ; it
is not cold calculation : it is study to ascertain that which is most
fit, and then ever-present will to announce the conclusion and urge
it forward for consideration.

Is it to be supposed that these persons did not understand that
their comfort would be promoted by silence and acquiescence ?

In neighborly intercourse I will bring you facts composing an
entire narrative in which I am deeply interested. I state them with
care, and from the manuscript or memory that my labor has made
absolutely correct. "What do you think about them ?" If I get
your opinion I am repaid for my toil. I am, in fact, your debtor.

And you in return will, by and by, come to me with such a matter of history or personal inquiry, having a like purpose. If there are no opinions to be given until a Round-robbin has been subscribed by all the villagers, then you and I want to leave the village. Not a boisterous, but a bold, candid opinion is required.

It is to be observed with respect to those who are frank and full in the utterance of their own well-considered opinions, that they are the most catholic and charitable. This is presumed and inevitable, when we say that their opinions are the result of judicious deliberation. And it seems to follow naturally from this, that persons of the character described give the best exhibitions of friendship ; are the most helpful to the young and the comparatively feeble and inexperienced, and are utterly devoid of all that species of morbid introspection which vitiates a vast amount of otherwise valuable energy in the world of mankind.

In localities where there are no citizens of strongly marked individuality, there is a breeding in and in of ideas, productive of mental imbecility and moral stagnation. And if there be faults inevitably connected with such characters, then it may be said that it is for the physical and mental healthfulness of the world that these infirmities be kindly recognized and everywhere exercised.

A multitude of thoughts, in argument and illustration crowd upon the mind in dwelling upon such a theme. But I admonish myself of the unusual amount of time in which I have kept your gracious and perfect attention.

Let us trust that this structure will long continue to ornament the village and accommodate the general public, and promote the common welfare.

My friends : I know it is your desire to enter as heartily into the sentiment of this dedication, as do we who sit and stand upon this platform to-night. Twenty years ago our father delivered a lecture in this village, in which he expressed regret that there was not a suitable hall for public convocation in the village. How providentially has he filled his judgment, and built his monument, and named a memorial.

This audience chamber is your legacy; not ours alone. And you have come, I think, to join in these ceremonies with unqualified interest and approval. And you will come to-morrow, and to-morrow, and to-morrow, as the appointments here shall be pleasing to you; each time sanctifying the place with your renewed tribute of regard and regret. Not with funereal melancholy; not as to a compelled service of commemoration,—like the Chinese, gathering around their mausoleums, to mourn for their ancestors of centuries gone by. The rays of his genial temperament shall beam upon you as you ascend the entrance steps. And a glance at her fair face shall dispel every thought of gloom. If you knew her, it shall enhance your appetite for cheerful song and decent mirth a hundred-fold.

Come! Come ye who were here before our father took his place among the citizens of the village. Come ye who knew him in his youthful days; who remember when he was first introduced in the town, and plead his first cause in John Hopkins' Court. Come! Come Isaac Seeley, and John and Asa Russell, and Ralph Taylor, and E. P. Woodworth, and B. W. Patterson, and Harvey Holmes, and Gilbert Munson, and Gideon Whiting, and the scores of co-temporaries that remain. Come! O! you knew the man. Come! And it cannot be otherwise than that without detracting from the special gratification that may be set for the hour, you will be largely recruited by the accessories and associations of the place, peculiar to your memories alone.

And ye widowed matrons and honored spinsters, whose neighborly intimacy began with him and his household through the wife of his youth, and has continued through the loving and faithful counsellor and deeply bereaved companion of his later years : Come!

And come, honest yeoman, old client : whom I have seen so often in the office, unrolling an old-fashioned pocket book, and taking out the long bank bill, for which you obtained a dollar's worth of legal lore : Come ! You know you had a well-earned equivalent for your money ; and the interest of your hard-earned fee is wrought into the texture of these walls, for your benefit and for the good of your children. Come !

Come ye lawyers : when on your occasional business trips through this section of the valley, there seems to be an invitation also in the entertainment that is here announced. Come ! You who have so often heard him rapidly rehearse the facts of his case with most unerring accuracy ; grouping them with unsurpassed skill in their most potential order ; and then focalizing and driving them home with terrible strength of logic and of sentiment : Come ! There is healthful professional tonic for you in the salubrious breezes that are wafted between these cornice windows. Come !

Ye who have heard him narrate the laughable facts, as only he could recite them : eliciting the ludicrous from the driest story ; dissecting a hypocrite with pitiless surgery, and reconstructing him in the picture with his contradictions in new joints,—provoking by the operation a fever of merriment, that at times seemed almost insufferable : Come !

And ye that have seen him—perchance gone with him—as, one after another he followed his three little children, and then his wife, to yonder cemetery : Come ! And come ye who have been with him beside the dying bed, or the grave of that daughter who had grown to womanhood, so lovely and so rich in promise,—" O, my only remaining daughter ! my child ! my child ! O Julia, my child ! would to God I could have died for thee !" Ye who have seen this strong man bowed down to earth by the afflictions with which the great enemy is still permitted to grievously wound the world of humanity, and know what tenderness there was in his nature : Come !

And every maiden who laid a flower on the old man's casket, and the unknown friend who secretly planted the green turf around his grave : Come !

All disagreements, all angerments—if a faint trace of any such abide—are to be dismissed to-night, and henceforth. Come ! The

10

old man as he went fearlessly down into the grave, closed his work in behalf of us all. He repented him of his faults in dust and ashes—as all men of his stamp and moral triumphs do: knowing that there is an advocate with the Father, who is sufficient for that which is lacking. And he bequeathed this edifice as a consummation of liberality and good-will to you. And now let us rise and join in the formal and ample dedication of this chamber, even as he devised and decreed it should be.

May it be a radiating centre of civilization and refinement, so long as its walls shall stand. May peace, and joy, and gladness, have a home in this secular tabernacle, and may the blessings and benedictions that carry all those good and gentle influences which father and daughter desired and delighted to exert, rest upon every one who shall gather here for a season of instruction, recreation, or benevolent counsels. As the new people and the new generations of the village pass by its portals, may they often be given a recollection of the dead, who cannot but speak most impressively to ancient acquaintances and friends in this pleasant structure ; all thankful that he found it in his heart to rear this building, ere his days were numbered ; accepting and carrying out his dying baptismal directions concerning his own memorial work ; thankful that these two lived to help and grace the virtuous society of the world ; praising God for the dispensation that set this man and this daughter in this valley ; repeating with emotions, it may be with tears, of love and pride, and emulating hope, the names of INCREASE and JULIA SUMNER.

www.ingramcontent.com/pod-product-compliance
Lightning Source LLC
Chambersburg PA
CBHW030017030726
47499CB00008B/3038